First Paperback Edition. Press.

ISBN (Paperback): 978-1-7358735-0-3
ISBN (E-book): 978-1-7358735-1-0

Disclaimer: The events and conversations in this book have been set down to the best of the author's ability, although some individuals' names and details have been changed to preserve their anonymity.

REVIEWS ARE THE LIFEBLOOD OF THIS NOVEL

IT'S A WAY FOR ME TO HEAR YOUR THOUGHTS SO I CAN STRIVE TO IMPROVE MY FUTURE WORK. IF YOU ENJOYED READING THIS NOVEL, PLEASE LEAVE AN *HONEST* REVIEW.

YOUR IMPACT IS *EXTRAORDINARY.*

For Isabel

Chapter 1

When I think about myself, I tend to think about the things I hate. It's a hefty list, coupled with a pessimistic attitude: my poor eyesight, my awful seasonal allergies, my two discolored buck teeth, my persistent dandruff, my skinny arms. It reads like a child's Christmas unwish-list.

But over time as you grow older, you forget to care about these faults— these daily physical reminders that you, like everyone else, has flaws and imperfections in some way or another. You just accept them.

And I have. But before, I used to wake up each morning thinking about these imperfections until I decided to hate different parts of myself. Parts you couldn't just "fix" with Lasik, a Claritin tablet, a retainer, a medically prescribed shampoo, or proper bicep curls.

No. They were *indomitable*. And painful. So painful that I wished I could chisel them off like imperfections on a marble statue. A hideous goatee left on the David of Michelangelo or a coagulated marble booger dripping out the nose of Discobolus.

I kept these pains shrouded for a long time. I felt disoriented in this new environment we all inhabit. One that feels hackneyed and trite to share your pains and struggles with the world. Before, we scurried around like hermit crabs, nestling our pinkish and vulnerable bodies tightly in our shells, burrowing our bodies along with our problems in the sand. But now, we wait in line in assembly-line fashion for our turn to approach the spotlighted microphone on stage to compete in a new game show— *America's Got Sadness!*

I really had pain, but there was no lesion or fracture I could attend to. The pain had no body. Instead, it was deep and existential. Every day for the past two years, I'd wake up and wallow in bed with the same thoughts— *Who am I? Why am I so alone? What do I believe?*

Today was no exception.

It's the same routine every morning. I wake up, huck out a yellow-colored loogie, cook two scrambled eggs (no cheese, since the Trader Joe's employee told me it was as addictive as crack cocaine), and open my phone. I try to make sure my blinding phone screen isn't the first thing I look at when I wake up.

Today, I received a *very* premature *Happy birthday I love you,* text from my mom. My birthday wasn't for another few weeks. I didn't have a party or anything special for it scheduled, nor would I actually plan one. I disliked the undeserved fanfare. Aside from my mom showing up to the party before the cake was even ordered, my inbox was usually empty.

If it's a weekday, I'll go to work. No messing around when it comes to my job. I'm in a fortunate position where I enjoy what I do.

Weekends are a different story. I'll mess around on my phone or watch YouTube videos until my eyes start to feel like they had contact lenses in them for the past month.

I would habitually flash my phone on— *0 MESSAGES IN YOUR INBOX.* This was typical, since I don't get out much. I don't see people often. I don't get invited to many places— at least, less now than before.

I know that friends are much more than a grey speech bubble in your phone asking if you're free to grab drinks at a local dive bar or take a road trip up to hike up the granite rocks of Yosemite. People are busy— and forgetful. Sometimes, I forget they have lives, too.

But I spend too much time at home, by myself, craving an invitation or a plan so I can feel some sort of community. Since this doesn't happen often, I try to leave my apartment as much as I can before I've pulled all the hair out of my scalp or strained my eyes from watching too many videos online. Usually, I'll go to a coffee shop or a public park . . . or, in today's case, a fancy college housing complex with an enormous study section.

Usually, when I do work on the weekend, I'm working on some passion pursuit I've enveloped myself in on the side of my job or schoolwork. I've had fleeting passion pursuits throughout college and several years later. Some were ambitious (running a sports tech company) and others absurd (training to be a close-up magician), but today, I was focused on my job.

I build applications on a cloud-based software and I was studying for a certification to show employers that I wasn't just a blindfolded monkey throwing darts at a dartboard. I actually *knew* what I was doing. I enjoy my work and the people I work with, which made studying that much easier.

The fancy college housing complex requires you to flash your apartment key (a black fob key with six dotted impressions on it) to the concierge at the front desk so while back, I borrowed a friend's and 3D-printed a replica. The concierge glances at it and barely recognizes the difference.

After I wolfed down my two (cheese-less) scrambled eggs and watched a good two hours of clips of *The Larry Sanders Show* on YouTube, I hopped in my 2005 black Acura MDX (cleverly named the *BLACK-ura* with 166,254 miles) and drove over to the complex. I always start the commute with an exhale. An exhale that says, *Another day, another monotony. Are you working on yourself today? Or is it something else?*

Today was cloudy, which was rare for Los Angeles, especially for a Sunday in August. The roads were quiet, so I was zooming through stop lights as if they didn't exist. Finally, I hit a red. I popped a peppermint in my mouth and glanced over at my phone. Nothing had changed, unsurprisingly. *0 MESSAGES IN YOUR INBOX.*

It's a sight I've just become numb to.

I left my car in the Popeye's parking lot, two blocks away from the complex. Parking was reserved for students, and my Photoshop skills weren't decent enough to fabricate a believable parking pass (or even a functioning one that could also open the gate).

It's the same routine here. I walk in with a, *Yes, I live here and pay the enormous rent,* confidence and flash the concierge my faux key. For double safety, I usually wear a T-shirt with the college logo and bring the backpack I used in college. The concierge nods and continues clacking on his keyboard.

I entered the study wing and found an open and cozy desk spot in the back corner. I dropped my backpack on the floor, pulled out my laptop, and waited for it to boot up. I analyzed the room. Lines of desk spaces were stretched throughout the vast hall in assembly-line fashion, as if they were designed by the Ford Motor Company. Each space was divided by plastic barriers, and nestled in each space was an overworked and under-rested college student, staring at their luminous computer screen.

My laptop hummed and flashed its home screen. I stared at the landscape photo of the sun beaming a bronze glow over the summit of the granite monolith, El Capitan. I hesitated to open my study notes. Usually, I could dive in with no problem, but today felt different.

I flashed on my phone screen again— *0 MESSAGES IN YOUR INBOX.* I let out a gentle sigh and turned it off. The past few years have been jarring to my psyche.

I graduated from a top university with a degree that had *zero* applicable skills to the real world. I took an entry-level sales job making $1,500 a month. Since LA rent would inevitably eat my entire monthly pay stub, I moved home with my father. He worked at his allergy practice during the day and came home at night to watch sports and finish his chicken piccata lunch from The Cheesecake Factory, courtesy of the high-heeled, platinum blonde pharmaceutical reps.

I liked my sales job at first. I hated sales, but my co-workers made it enjoyable. They had Boston bar-type humor— crass and offensive— which made them easier to play conversational tennis with.

However, as time went on, sales went from disinteresting to poisonous, so I quit. I worked in retail and walked dogs to make money until I found a new job– one I enjoyed. I could finally afford my own apartment. I could finally sustain myself.

I pursued some passion projects on the side. All of them failed or fizzled out, just as they did in college. My social circle shrank. Friends left the city for new careers, lives, and experiences. Some got married, while others furthered their education. My LinkedIn was flooded with future doctors, lawyers, MBA holders, PhD candidates, you name it. I was doggie-paddling in molasses.

How big was this bowl?

At the time, I was content. However, I had been in pain for most of my life without any real thought about it. I never stopped to think about it until I finally did.

Two years ago, I was sitting in my newly inhabited apartment. A quaint two-bedroom with granite countertops and stainless steel appliances. A sub-par halogen-bulb chandelier hung over an assembled black IKEA coffee table with a "Welcome to your new home!" letter from management. Nothing else was set up; I had a mattress on the wooden floor surrounded by cardboard boxes with illegible labels scribbled on the sides (courtesy of my father's doctoral handwriting). I was carrying the final box into my bedroom when a flurry of thoughts rushed into my head.

Is this what you want? Is this who you are? Where are your friends? Where is your community? What do you believe in? Are you happy? Fulfilled? Is this a good life? Is this the life you want to live?

I dropped the box and slumped my body down to the floor. To this day, I still can't seem to tackle the catalyst for these questions, nor can I properly answer them, which created a pain inside of me. Maybe it was the sudden shift in my life and seeing everything I owned in cardboard boxes waiting to be unopened.

Should I open them here or somewhere else?

Those questions were vital, and I had no hint, inkling, or clue of how to answer them. I had been in pain ever since that moment, as if the morphine IV that had pumped its numbing goodness into my veins for the past 25 years was suddenly yanked out of my arm.

I didn't feel like myself. I didn't know what part of me was authentic and what was fabricated. I felt alone in a world with seven billion others who could share the same emotions and DNA as mine. I felt like my belief system had been damaged and disarranged, dying for a proper recalibration.

Then, I sat back in my chair. I looked at my desktop. El Capitan was still glowing from the bright glow of the sun. Out of the corner of my eye, a file on my computer caught my attention— a Word document titled "Journal." I hovered my mouse over the paper icon and double-clicked. The document filled my computer screen.

—JOURNAL ENTRY 1—

November 4, 2018

I recently picked up a copy of Fahrenheit 451 with a new foreword by Neil Gaiman. I've been binge-watching his recorded speaking events on YouTube and he quickly became my writing muse, but I revered him even more after reading his foreword. In it, he describes the three phrases that allow us to write about what he calls the "world of not-yet."

What if . . . ?

If only . . .

If this goes on . . .

I thought about these three phrases. And I thought about myself. While Neil was talking about the science or speculative fiction of the world (what if . . . aliens came and attacked our world, but they weren't aliens at all— they were us!) I read them as the speculative fiction of myself. The speculative fiction of my life and the things I want to fix.

What if . . . I had the ability to fix my pain.

If only . . . I could live a better life, one free of current misery.

If this goes on . . . things will get worse. Much worse.

Parts of my life are painful, but this pain hasn't always been in my life. Pain itself is ubiquitous. Some experience more, while others experience less. Some experience more in the beginning, and others experience more in the end.

So let's start at the beginning, where I had a rather swift introduction to pain when my 16-month-old brother dropped me on the back of my head when I was just eight minutes old. I don't think that's the primary reason for why I feel so different, but I often wonder what the ceramic-tiled floor did to my mushy brain.

I paused. "Mushy" felt like a basic adjective to use here. I put my fingers on the keyboard and began to edit.

. . . the ceramic-tiled floor did to my ~~mushy~~ semiliquid brai—.

I paused again. *"No you idiot,"* I thought to myself. *"You're getting too scientific. Stop trying to use big words to make it seem like you're smarter than you actually are."*

I've been told all my life that I was the smart one, the one in the family with intelligence. But I saw intelligence as a curse; an inability to live in blissful ignorance. I lifted my fingers from the keyboard for a moment before returning them.

. . . the ceramic-tiled floor did to my ~~semiliquid~~ Play-Doh-like brain.

That looked better. When in doubt, humor is always the great equalizer between intelligence and stupidity.

I'll admit, it felt weird at first to write my journal on a laptop. No leather-bound Moleskine by my side; no delicate fountain pen that glided the ink onto the pages like a paintbrush; no lit candles; and certainly no steaming cup of coffee. I don't even drink coffee. Too much caffeine for me and I'm already as annoying as is without the journalists' favorite stimulant.

However, I still couldn't answer my painful questions, and they kept resurfacing. They became impossible to ignore, but remained vague and nebulous.

"How do I accurately and authentically fix these pains in my life?"

My friend suggested I journal, but instead of writing about the present, I should write about the past . . . about memorable parts of my life. How they happened, and what (if any) significance they held. Like a retro Atari game, they could hold some clues or secrets that I wouldn't see at first glance.

I made solid progress. It even turned into a weekly ritual, like celebrating the Shabbos or the end of the work week with Moscow mules and drunkenly peeing on the side of a temple on the walk home (despite that being sacrilegious). Every Sunday night, I would make a cup of caffeine-free herbal tea, sit outside on my balcony at a flimsy wooden patio table, allow the tainted LA air fill my lungs, and write about the first event from my past that came to mind. My balcony was made of some type of mysterious rock and was only illuminated by a tiny halogen lightbulb. The brightness of the white Word document often strained my eyes.

Why do I do that instead of just writing inside, where it's lighter, warmer, more breathable, and less eye strain? No clue. It just became my ritual. I mean, why do we leave warm milk and freshly baked cookies out for a fat stranger to come down our chimney at night and deliver us presents? It's a ritual. Stop asking questions and just say, "*Merry Christmas.*"

It's been nine months and my journal (Word document) has beefed up to about 40 pages, filled with memories about my childhood, my time in college, my professional career, and sprinkles of disjointed experiences, that for some reason, I have a rather clear memory of. These experiences were written in front of me, but I didn't know what to do with them. I still didn't know how to use them to fix the pains in my life. My journal hasn't helped me so far.

My stomach growled, so I dug into my backpack looking for the lemon energy bar I packed this morning to distract my appetite. I blindly rummaged around the bottom, using my fingers to feel something mushy and rectangular.

I couldn't find it. I lifted my backpack off the ground out of frustration while the front pouch was open, flipped it upside down, and poured everything on the carpet floor in front of me. My backpack was full of excess crap— extra paper, sticky notes, a ruler, a broken Ticonderoga pencil, a bike lock, my green comb, an unlatched silver stainless steel carabiner, extra contact solution, and a deck of cards— but no lemon energy bar. I collected everything off the floor and stuffed it in my backpack. I unzipped the smaller pouch. It only had a copy of Daniel Quinn's *Ishmael* and a bottle of hand sanitizer. Still, no lemon power bar. I zipped my backpack up and leaned back in my chair.

I looked at the time on my phone. 2:23 pm. *The security guard is about to make another round in seven minutes.* My faux key works with the other 14 guards on staff, but this particular patroller caught me two years prior. Before I snuck in to use the study space, I used the key to take advantage of their other amenities: pools, hot tubs, arcade room, a gym with a climbing wall, and two full-sized indoor basketball courts. This particularly staunch patroller caught me while playing basketball after a friend let me in the backside of the complex, since I left my faux key at home.

I was shooting around, minding my own business, when he begrudgingly walked down the flight of stairs to the basketball court. He shot me a look dirtier than a plumber's utility belt and asked me where my key was. I couldn't present one, so he started to grill me, asking if I was a resident (*"Well if you live here, then you obviously have an apartment number. What's your apartment number?"*) I didn't have a key or an apartment number, so he asked for my driver's license.

"It's a pleasure to meet you, Sam," he read off my license with a faint chuckle. "Don't worry, I'll remember your face if you ever sneak into here again. You can bet on that." He escorted me out, and now, *he knows my face.*

I packed up my belongings and headed for the bathroom. I sat in the stall and took a deep breath. I started to stress as a swell of anxiousness carried over my body. I started twirling my hair, knotting the strands together, and pulling them out until I realized what I was doing. I swatted my hand away with the other. When a habit becomes so subconscious, it's hard to premeditatively stop. I opened my backpack to find my green comb missing, so I used my fingers to slick and rake my hair back when my phone started to buzz.

Security guard check - use side bathroom.

Nice, I was ahead of my own security alerts. Two sets of shoes entered the bathroom stall. One went for the urinal and the other washed his hands in the sink. I waited in the stall for them to leave. The tiled floor and glass mirrors echoed their conversation well enough for me to hear. One of them talked about a new clothing line he was launching soon. The other talked about his abhorrent pre-med classes and how he wanted to switch his major to economics and head east to Wall Street.

I don't trust people who talk about their life exclusively in the present or future tense. When I hear things like, "I'm working on this project," or "I'm going to build this," or "I'm starting this new venture," they all say to me, "I haven't finished!"

But here I am, acting like a complete cynic– the pessimism of my own life seeping into my vision of others.

The two sets of feet left through the double-swinging door. I flashed on my phone screen. 2:41 pm.

I think I'm in the clear. I walked back to my desk to see it taken by an actual student. *What an asshole*, I thought to myself, as if *I* wasn't the asshole taking spots away from these hardworking students.

But I was pissed. I always sat at that desk. It was wedged in the corner of the library and had the furthest distance between all the other desks. I liked my personal space.

I stormed in anger over to the small cafe that served salad wraps and chicken tenders to the overworked and under-rested college students. I sat in the most isolated booth in the seating area and opened up my laptop to be greeted by the sound of a customer service bell that was just smacked by an impatient hotel guest.

A notification banner popped up on my screen that read:

Time to Journal!!!

The exclamation marks seemed excessive now. When I made the notification, I was excited about something new. Something that could give me insight or enlightenment into my life. That was, of course, a while ago.

I closed the alarm. *Why even try?* Two years of unanswered questions, nine months of journaling, and 40 pages of experiences without a single catharsis. It felt like the melancholy music playing in the background of my life started to crescendo so I could finally hear it . . . and the music was cacophonic.

I didn't want to continue living in this deep reservoir of resentment, leaving these parts of my life unchecked, but I was mentally exhausted. I had hit an awful roadblock with no way of maneuvering around it. I sat there watching the students devour chicken Caesar wraps and pizza slices. Then, a possible four-leaf clover appeared.

My phone buzzed and I immediately tapped the home screen— *1 NEW MESSAGE*. It was a text from my brother:

Answer your damn phone.

I checked my missed calls. He didn't show up. Then, my phone started buzzing in my hand. He was calling me. I accepted and lazily secreted the words, "Hey, what's up," out my mouth.

"Are you sitting in front of your computer?" he asked.

There was no "Hey" or "How are you doing" to start the call. He got straight to the point. I told him I was.

"Good," he concluded. "I'm buying you a plane ticket. I need you to put in your info."

I was confused at first. Adam wasn't someone I'd label as altruistic with something as expensive as a roundtrip plane ticket. He was a year and a half older than me.

Our facial features were eerily similar– we both had thick eyebrows and coarse dark black hair, with short haircuts that didn't go past three inches. We grew up like most brothers do, kicking the ever-living crap out of each other. Punching, fighting, wrestling, putting accidental holes in the drywall . . . it was all there for my mom to deal with, whose jaw occasionally dropped to the floor.

In one instance, I was tying my shoes in an awkward position when he decided to sit on top of me, spraining my leg. Another time, he took my favorite fire truck, so I chased him around my aunt's house until I ran into the corner of a glass table. The doctor put in a few stitches right above the corner of my right eyebrow and gave me a lollipop. (I still have the battle scar, but not the firetruck.)

He has sprained my knee, bruised my tailbone, and dragged my naked back across the carpet numerous times. I was the weaker one, but I wasn't always the victim. One time, I took a wooden bat to his stones, and now, I'd say we're even-stevens.

But we'll never be. *Brothers always fight.*

After college, he worked in sales at what exploded into a unicorn tech company. The company's booming success and his impeccable sales skills sent him to live overseas in Australia to expand the EMEA market. After setting footprints in New Zealand, Thailand, Cambodia, Singapore, and Korea (the south one), he returned to the states and settled in a high rise in downtown San Diego. I would be lying if I told you that my initial stab at pursuing a sales career wasn't influenced by him. But now, here he was, offering me a free (and expensive) roundtrip ticket.

"Where are we going?" I asked.

He ignored my question. "Can you take some days off work?"

I told him I could.

"We finally have an opportunity to visit her," he said. "Our parents are never going to go, so we might as well make the trip."

I hate surprises, so I asked him where we were going.

And then I learned it was somewhere unique. Somewhere I thought I would never go in my life. Then, a flurry of new thoughts entered my head.

I'll finally have a chance to see her. I finally get to visit a special place to see someone special. I'll finally get to do what no one in my family has done.

My body stood still for a moment. In a second, nothing else mattered. I dropped everything and shifted my focus to booking my ticket online.

This could change everything.

6 DAYS FROM DEPARTURE

The room was pitch black. At least, I thought I was in a room. I took a few cautious steps, each one creating a crunching and crackling sound of dirt, rocks, sand, and sticks.

This was no room.

A white glow illuminated the corner of my eye– a perfectly circular light with splotches of dark grey. I looked around the field of tall corn stalks and dead grass. No civilization around. No cities. An area devoid of needing resources imported. An area that's completely self-sustaining. I could feel my recent reading of Derrick Jensen impacting my perception.

The light illuminated the area around me, but I couldn't see far enough in the distance, so I walked. More crunching and crackling.

The air was hot and humid. I looked up to see no clouds and no stars, just more darkness. The ground became elevated, and I was suddenly walking uphill. I didn't feel tension in my legs. I didn't feel the exercise. I just kept walking.

The perfectly circular light shone brighter and I could see more with every step I took. I could see small shrubs in the distance, trying so hard to stay green around the tall brown grass. I could see a faint outline of a mountain range in the distance. At least, that's what it looked like. The land was littered with short growing vegetation. There was only one tree, further up the hill. Its branches swayed as the hot, humid hair blew through. Pink flower petals fell and landed delicately among the dead brown short grass.

And then, the perfectly circular light shone into my eyes.

I opened my eyes and realized I was in a waiting room with fluorescent-panel lights blinding my eyes and beige colored walls with paintings you'd typically see in a nursing home. The walls were lined with display cases of different types of glasses. Two other patients sat in flimsy plastic chairs with checkered colored cushions.

An old man was sitting next to me. He tapped me on the shoulder with his thin, spindly fingers, like spires on a cathedral.

Why the hell did you wake me up?

I compartmentalized my anger and gave him a smarmy grin. He smiled back and nodded. I was surprised that he didn't smack the entitled-millennial smirk off my face.

"Sam," a voice from the other side of the room said. "Dr. Harding will see you now." The nurse was standing by the door holding a wooden clipboard.

I must have zoned out in my dream. For how long? Probably awhile. Long enough for the old man to poke me with his needle-point Nosferatu fingers. I'm surprised I didn't have a fully-grown depression-era beard by then.

I stuffed my laptop in my bag and followed her through the door. I said hello to the cute receptionist sitting behind the large opaque desk as I passed by. She gave a half-hearted smile without showing her teeth.

She led me into his patient room, where I sat in a chair in front of a phoropter— the clunky steampunk-looking instrument that eye doctors make you look through to determine how crappy your vision is. I planned on a short visit; all I needed was an eye exam to buy more contacts.

"He'll be in shortly, just hang tight," she said, shutting the door and entering back into the hallway of buzzing opticians. The slam from the door was jarring as it echoed throughout the room.

I glanced around the room in boredom. The snow white walls were stacked with cabinets, with semi-transparent glass covering them. A plush elephant sat on top of a computer monitor accompanied by a keyboard and a chair with wheels. Shelves were filled with books and files.

I turned my attention to the top shelf, where I could see the names of a few books written on the spine. I squinted my eyes to make out the titles. *The Neuro-Ophthalmology Survival Guide,* one read. I read another: *Ocular Therapeutics Handbook: A Clinical Manual.* A third sat on top of the other two, colored with a white spine and a greenish gradient on the bottom. *Aix Galericulata,* the title read.

My examination of the room was then interrupted by two knocks at the door. The door opened and Dr. Harding walked in, shook my hand, and took a seat by the blank monitor. He dressed more like an English professor than an optometrist. He wore a dark blue V-neck sweater with a checkered shirt underneath, blue jeans, and brown suede shoes. It was a more casual look compared to the white coat and optical trial framed glasses I was used to seeing. He flipped through some pages on a wooden clipboard.

"Okay, so it looks like you just need an eye exam," he said while keeping his gaze on the pages. He spoke softly like he was always wearing a cardigan or a corduroy blazer with leather elbow pads. I smiled and nodded at him. He started to type away on the keyboard connected to the computer monitor.

"I'm going on a trip next week," I told him. "It's going to be sunny over there, and I want to wear my sunglasses."

"I see," he said while keeping his attention in front of the computer. After a few moments, he stopped typing and rolled his chair over to me. He grabbed the phoropter by the handle and swiveled it in front of my face.

"Just a formality, but I need to know if you are experiencing any of the following symptoms: Eyestrain?"

"No."

"Itchy eyes?"

"Nope."

"Fluctuating vision?"

"No."

"Any headaches?"

"Nada. I just need the eye exam so I can get a prescription to pick up contacts at Costco."

He smiled and instructed me to put my face up against the phoropter. "I gotcha," he said. "I've never been down there in my life, but I heard it's nice this time of year. You'll need sunglasses."

The letters on the eye chart were flickered in front of my eyes. After a few correct (and incorrect) guesses from looking at blurry and sharp letters on the chart, he pulled the phoropter away from my face and swiveled his chair back to the computer. He started typing away, so I took another glance around his office. Nothing out of the ordinary. Shelves of books. Cabinets filled with tools. A wall calendar with a picture of a poppy flower for August. A metal sink in the corner with a bottle of contact solution sitting on the edge of the bowl.

I glanced over at the bookshelf and noticed a square object leaned up against its side. I got up to wash my hands in the sink to get a better view. I could make out the writing on the paper framed inside. It looked like a medical degree.

This man has an identity, I thought to myself. He could go to bars, fancy dinners, networking events, decorated galas, and tell people with confidence, "I'm a doctor."

He had something I desperately wish I had. And there it was, on the ground, and out of sight like an unwanted birthday present.

"I'd hang that on the wall next to the poppy calendar if I had that," I jokingly said, glancing over at the degree on the floor leaning up against the bookshelf. He smiled but didn't respond. I finished washing my hands and sat back in the chair. He typed on the computer for a few more minutes before swiveling his chair over to me. He had me open the eyelids on my right eye while he shone a bright light into my pupil.

"You know," he said in a lecturing tone while waving the light across my pupil. "The eye is the most complex organ in our body." He looked into my pupil and hummed to himself for a moment.

"Aside from our brain, of course."

He instructed me to do the same with my left eye. I opened my eyelids and he shone the light in my pupil. "The machines in our body that help us see and perceive the world around us are more complex than the machines we use to operate in it. Isn't that fascinating!"

He flashed the light for a few more seconds before flipping it off. He swiveled his chair back to the computer and started typing on the keyboard. "It's a little worse on the left side," he concluded. "I'll bump you up to -2.75 and you'll be on your way."

I was still curious. *Why the hell would you leave your medical degree on the floor?* I prodded him further.

"Have you thought about displaying your degree?"

He typed on the keyboard and avoided eye contact with me. I prodded him again.

"Wouldn't you want to hang it up?"

"It's not mine," he finally responded. I reserved myself and shifted my tone to sound less intrusive.

"Oh, I didn't know. I just assumed—"

"It's okay. It's a fair assumption. But it's not mine. It was my father's."

We sat in silence for a moment. The room was filled with the sound of the keyboard keys clacking. I prodded further.

"And you don't want to hang it up on the wall?"

He sighed. "I didn't have a need to."

Again, we paused in silence for a moment but this time, he stopped typing on the keyboard.

"Was he also a doctor?" I asked.

"Yes, but not like me."

"What was he?"

"A different kind. A surgeon."

"Oh."

A third silence fell over the room. He went back to clacking the keyboard keys. "You know," he said. "We were both on the same path at one point in our lives."

"And you didn't want to follow him?" I asked.

"I did for a while, but I had a different path in mind."

"But the other seems more lucrative."

Dr. Harding paused and pulled away from his computer. He swiveled his chair over and asked me to put my face back up to the phoropter. I brought my face forward and aligned my eyes to look through the two eye holes covered with a glass lens.

"Not all roses in the garden carry the same scent," he said while adjusting and calibrating the measures on the phoropter. He brought his eyes in line with mine on the other side of the eye holes.

"So why didn't you follow him?" I nudged.

Dr. Harding twirled a widget on the bottom of the phoropter, making my vision sharper while looking through the eye holes. I kept looking at an image of a hot air balloon floating above a desert floor inside the phoropter.

"Working 100 hours a week from opening chest cavities and attending medical conferences takes a toll on a man— and his family. He was never home. I rarely saw him. He never showed me how to throw a baseball or fix things in the house."

This time, I tried to sound more optimistic.

"But did he at least love what he did? I mean, saving people's lives must be a hell of a fulfilling career."

Dr. Harding pulled the phoropter away from my face. He swiveled his chair over to a drawer and pulled out a small sheet of paper. He grabbed a ballpoint pen from a drawer and started writing.

"He didn't," he retorted. He stopped writing to look up at my face still glued to the eye holes in the phoropter. "You can stop looking through that." I pushed it away from my face and he looked at me. His voice had gone up a few decibels and my face clearly showed it.

I saw a slightly disheveled look in his face. "I'm sorry if I prodded you on this," I told him. "I was curious. I didn't know it was so . . . personal."

He went back to writing on the sheet of paper. "It's okay." He jotted some illegible notes and grinned. "It's funny," he chuckled. "One day in college, he sat outside the library on a wooden bench waiting for me. I sat next to him. We didn't talk for a while until we did. He told me he never had any interest in what was inside of each of us. Hearts, livers, and kidneys all looked the same to him— no matter who they came from. Sure, they varied in shapes and sizes, but he told me that, to him, they all looked the same. Nothing unique about any of them. And every day, he would cut them out of people. He never told me why he found a job like that so discouraging. Maybe it was the monotony of the job or the long hours, but when he was speaking to me on that cold day, sitting on that freezing wooden bench, I could see that he never truly enjoyed it. I had been following his path all my life up until that point. Then I decided to pursue my own."

He finished writing my prescription on the small sheet of paper and handed it to me. "I'd go tomorrow. Costco marked down their contacts last week."

I took the piece of paper and folded it four times to stuff in my wallet. "I would still hang it up," I insisted. "He's still an important part of your life."

"He *was*," he corrected with affection and shook my hand. He smiled and I thanked him for his time.

I walked out of his office to my car and saw a bright yellow ticket on my windshield. The parking meter was flashing a bright red light like a homing beacon to all parking enforcement officers. I guess the story was a bit longer than I thought. I couldn't be mad. It's easy to make fun of a cop for riding a bike or yell at a meter maid for giving me a parking ticket, but all these people are earning their wealth–whether for my protection or suffering.

Just another monotonous event on a monotonous day in a monotonous life.

It was starting to sound like a jingle.

1 DAY FROM DEPARTURE

I sprawled my body over my bed. I wondered how many hours I had spent looking at my computer screen. My eyes watered with a ruby tint around the irises. A *ding* sound blared from my laptop with a banner message:

Time to Journal!!!

I stopped. I lifted my hands off my keyboard, put them behind my neck, and squeezed them together, flaring my elbows out.

I audibly groaned. Then, I got anxious. I started twirling my hair, knotting the strands together, and pulling them out. After a few moments, I smacked my hair-pulling hand with the other. I checked my backpack again and still couldn't find my comb. I pulled more strands of hair out of my scalp.

I hadn't had any decent human interaction since my appointment with Dr. Harding. When I don't talk to people for a long time, I'll stare into my bathroom mirror and speak gibberish, just to remind myself of how it feels to talk to another person. But tomorrow was a day I was excited for.

I closed the banner message on my laptop and glanced at my virtual calendar, with a four-day block titled "vacation."

But this wasn't a vacation. I wouldn't be sipping mojitos and iced bourbon by an infinity pool in Cabo, nor would I be rolling snake eyes in craps or carrying a handful of technicolored poker chips in Vegas.

No, we're going somewhere much different. Somewhere less lavish, but far more meaningful.

As the pain percolated to the surface once again, a flurry of thoughts entered my head.

After this trip ends, then what? What will you do next? You'll be back where you started. Who are you? Why are you so alone? What do you believe?

I shook my head and covered my eyes with my palms. The emotional and mental tolls of these unanswered questions— these unsolved pains— were sucking my life away like an existential leech.

I got up from my desk and walked into the kitchen. I opened my fridge to some eggs, almond milk, two green apples, pasta in a Ziploc bag (*why the hell is this in the fridge?*), and a jar of chunky peanut butter. I was clearly in dire need of a trip to the grocery store.

Yes, another monotonous task to eat up the time in your monotonous life.

I told the voice in my head to shut up.

I closed the fridge and draped myself over my frat-stained mattress. I looked over at the wall. Two months ago, I snagged a whiteboard from my company as they were clearing out their storage room. That same day, I drilled it into my wall, grabbed a Sharpie, and wrote *Relax* in black permanent ink (*What, are you a yogi now?*).

I've spent so much time thinking— actually, *over*thinking. I'd be dwelling in the past, but nervously waiting for the future. I didn't want to keep thinking. I wanted to sit back and enjoy things as they came, being present for events in real-time.

This trip wouldn't be about addressing my pains, it would be about suspending them for a brief period of time.

Tomorrow, I'll be 30,000 feet in the air, destined to arrive in a new place, completely unknown to me.

A place for me to find some peace and calmness.

A place for me to not think.

A place for me to simply observe.

This place is special– not to me, but to someone else, who's special to me. And that's what makes it special.

Adam called me earlier to make sure I had my ticket, passport, and suitcases packed. I had my ticket, my passport with a picture of prepubescent me was lying somewhere around the apartment, and my empty duffle back lay flat and deflated at the front of my door, waiting to be stuffed with my wrinkled, loose-fitting clothes.

He was excited, too. To see the same woman he cares so much about— the same amount I do.

Our parents would never make this trip out. We knew that. There's a lot of *uncertainty* with a trip like this. They preferred vacationing in comfort, and understandably so. Uncertainty can be unpleasant to some, but contrary to our bloodline, Adam and I bent in a completely different direction.

Chapter 2

"Man, I fucked up today."

That was my Uber driver, Martin, who was responsible for my safety. When I got into his beige 2005 Honda Odyssey, he started with a cordial boilerplate question, asking me how my morning was going. I responded and hot potato-ed the question back to him, and that's when he told me that he had fucked up.

I looked at him through the rearview mirror, and he definitely had the face of someone who had just fucked up. I decided to take a bite.

"What happened?" I asked.

He put his hands on the wheel at 10 and 2 as he exhaled. "I spent all night driving people around. Probably made about 200 bucks tops. Then I stopped at a gas station to piss and ended up spending it all on scratchers at the mini mart. I lost all my cash in a heartbeat."

He grabbed the failed scratchers stuffed in the lip of the car's sun visor and handed them to me for inspection. All of them were furiously scratched, with not even a cent of winnings to collect.

"Man, I'm still living paycheck to paycheck. I have two kids I need to feed. Goddamn, I messed up."

While I didn't plan on playing therapist at five in the morning in the backseat of an Uber, I felt like I had to say something. I've also been someone who has caved into bad habits that led to that pernicious afterthought— *Why the hell did I just do that?*

With habits that I didn't like, I tried to create the most amount of friction as possible, to the point where it became a nuisance to have to perform them. I used friction the most with video games. I would lock my games in a box and give them to my roommate, or I'd scatter the cords all over my apartment, so I'd have to go on a mini scavenger hunt before playing.

I told Martin about friction and how it might be effective in his situation. I even gave him some tips, like leaving his credit cards at home, or to avoid stopping at gas stations to piss, and instead use fast food chains. He laughed and said he never thought of something like that. He thought it was clever. I started to pick my hair.

We pulled up to the airport and I hopped out to get my luggage from his trunk. As I started to walk inside, Martin rolled down his window and called my name. His booming voice caught me off-guard, so my neck swiveled around, causing my body to almost perform a cartoonish pirouette.

"Hey man!" he yelled from the car window. "Take down my number. I'll pick you up when you get back."

He shouted his number and I punched it into my phone. I thanked him and told him I'd call him in a few days. He drove off— leaving tire marks on the concrete— and I entered the airport terminal.

———

The plane wheels kissed the tarmac at eight o'clock at night. We flew in a small carrier plane that could fit no more than 40 passengers. Nobody in our family had ever visited Oaxaca but I had a damn good reason to go: to see *My Second Mother*.

Her name was *Isabel*, and she had helped raise me and Adam for the first 12 years of our lives. She was there when I was being processed in the maternity ward and she was there when Adam was still having trouble eating solid foods. But too much time had passed and we hadn't seen her in a long time. This trip would be special for *everyone*.

The plane pulled into a lane on the tarmac and we were let off one by one. As I was getting off, I could see a large cloud pounding rain over a green-spattered mountain range. Adam exited first and I trailed behind, taking a good look at the cloud and the vessel we just flew on.

I took out my phone and eagerly snapped a picture of the cloud and the carrier plane when a crewmember told me to stop. Apparently, it was forbidden to take photos of the plane. I acted like a dumb American tourist and he gave me a sour look.

We got off the tarmac and walked through the security protocols. From the corner of my eye, I saw a motion-sensor sliding door.

As flight-goers went through the door, I spotted her standing on the other side, holding a giant set of welcome balloons with a gleeful smile on her face— *My Second Mother*.

Isabel was short in stature, standing just under five feet tall, but gave the warmest hugs out of anybody I knew. Her skin was dark brown, and her black hair was short and thin, like angel hair pasta, streaked with grey. You could see the skin on her scalp if you were looking down at her.

As we made eye contact, she ran over to me and Adam, giving us those incredibly warm hugs that we had always remembered. She spoke in a kind, yet jubilant tone, and her semi-fluent English created some endearing pronunciations and partially complete sentences that mixed perfectly with her Oaxacan accent.

"You grow so beeg, Sammy!"

She released me from the warm hug and scanned me up and down with her eyes. Her voice boomed with excitement.

"Why you get so beeg? You so tall now, why you so tall?"

Last time I saw Isabel I was probably 5'10." Now, I stood at a staggering five-foot-ten-and-a-*half* inches.

"He's finally eating, isn't that something?" Adam poked in while grabbing my stomach. I laughed and said nothing.

She was overjoyed to see both of us. Isabel's sister, Lupita, and her husband, Tony, had accompanied her to drive us back to the house, since Isabel didn't own a car. They only knew bits of English, but not enough to hold a conversation.

Isabel couldn't stop hugging us. We stayed in the airport for another 20 minutes before detaching and walking out to the parking lot.

Only 10 of the parking spots were filled. No trams, cabs, buses, shuttles, or frequent intercom announcements. It was deadly quiet, such a stark contrast to the airport I'm used to (LAX).

They had driven in a five-seater Volkswagen sedan, so we made ourselves comfortable. We packed inside. Adam and I sat in the two back seats, with Isabel continuing to hug us as she sat in between. I had never seen such excitement in her eyes.

"I never think in my entire life that 'ju would come!"

We drove from the airport through Santa Lucía del Camino, Tlacolula de Matamoros, and eventually to the small nearby town where Isabel lived— just shy of 40 kilometers away from Oaxaca City.

The commute back to Isabel's village was 40 minutes, so we spent the majority of the car ride telling Isabel about our lives.

"See," Adam said while flipping through photos on his phone to show Isabel. "There's the pool, gym, and oh, look at this. This is the giant movie theater-sized TV they have by the cabanas."

He had just moved into his new high-rise in San Diego. Isabel had never seen anything like it. I mean, a pool on a rooftop? That's ludicrous.

"You live in this one?" Isabel asked with amazement painted in her eyes, clutching his phone.

He chuckled and flashed his white teeth. "Yup, it's too much money, but I don't care."

The nearest rooftop pool in my life was at the Waldorf Astoria, and two nights there was half my rent. Isabel laughed from her stomach and rubbed her hand on his kneecap.

"You always like this expensive stuff! Your taste is *muy rico*!"

I disengaged myself from the conversation by looking out the window. Adam extended his arm over Isabel to tickle my armpit. I slapped his hand away, but still smiled reflexively. He gave me an *I'm your brother and I'm gonna annoy you all weekend* face.

Isabel turned back to Adam.

"I knew in the first minute you would start something!" She then turned her attention to me. "Sammy, just ignore this one. He's probably *borracho.*"

I looked at Adam, whose head was hovering behind Isabel's—snickering like a devious child planning to sneak out of his room to watch inappropriate midnight television. Isabel turned back to Adam and slapped his chest.

"I'm no *borracho!*" he whelped while simultaneously laughing. Isabel turned back to me.

"What's new, Sammy? How are you?"

I looked away from the window and back to Isabel. I was exceptional (borderline Olympic) at shrouding my problems by becoming a social chameleon. I was able to fabricate a personality or image for others to see and hide the things that were truly painful in my life. But I promised myself I would try to enjoy the moment.

"Things are great!" I said with forced enthusiasm. "My job is great, I love the people." This was actually true. "I've been spending a lot of time with friends, going out, and a bunch of other things." This part wasn't true.

Isabel smiled and rubbed my kneecap with her hand. The thought entered my head again. Now, it started to sound like a jingle.

Another monotonous drive on a monotonous day in a monotonous life.

Shut up!

I bludgeoned my pessimism for a moment and looked out the window. We finally arrived in Isabel's village— Villa Díaz Ordaz. After leaving the main road, the shops and restaurants (and fields of agave plants) on the side of the streets were replaced with farmland, dirt, and vegetation. Small patches of tall corn stalks and lemon trees were planted in some areas, while others let the natural growth of the plants and trees spring from the ground.

The distant horizon was bright blue, painted with the outline of the mountain peaks of Cerro Yatin and Cerro Zempoaltepetl. The pavement road quickly turned to dirt, as I could hear the rocks getting kicked up in the air from the tires of the car while thick brown clouds started to materialize from passing cars on the other side of the road.

Isabel started to explain the activities that we would do during our three-day trip. Her plan was perfect for any tourist, but at the age of 65, I didn't want to tire her out with 15-hour-long days. I tried to suggest activities that required less energy, but she shot them down.

"Sammy, I'm used to 'dees lifestyle."

I had to agree— her life was anything but relaxed.

———

Isabel was loving, kind, sweet, ebullient, and charismatic, but she wasn't given much to start with. She was born in a rural village in Oaxaca and raised in a small hut made of mud and sticks. She hadn't experienced electricity until the age of 15 and would be (un)happily married a year later.

Until she was 36, Isabel remained in an abusive relationship with a husband who would constantly beat her within an inch of death. She suffered from insomnia due to the erratic behavior she was subjected to, but after 20 years, she left him and made the pilgrimage to America to escape his grip and find work.

Her childhood made her tough like a well-done rib eye, but when she finally stepped foot on American soil, she was filled with depression and hate. She felt like the world had betrayed her, thinking that everything around her was so vicious and vile. She thought about why God would make her live such a life. She had always been nice, fair, caring, and loving— *why was she given this life?*

She initially found work in southern California, but lost her job after the 1994 Northridge earthquake that ravaged the city. She shifted her focus and started looking for a position to work with children. After looking for work as a nanny for quite some time, she finally met a nice couple living in Los Angeles with a one-year-old boy that kept them busy and had another one on the way.

When I was born in Los Angeles, Isabel was there. My parents were living with each other while Isabel frequently came over to help as a nanny. At the time, we didn't have room in our house for her to stay, so every day, her commute involved taking three different bus lines and walking over three miles to get to our house— a total of three hours from her place to ours.

When I was only a year old, my aunt was diagnosed with a rare form of cancer, so my mother moved north to Washington to be with her. Adam, Isabel, and I went with her, while our father stayed behind to keep his business running. He would commute almost every Thursday by flight to visit us and go back to Los Angeles on Sunday to get ready for work.

By that point, Isabel had a room to herself so she wouldn't have to commute, but all day and night, she had to deal with me and Adam constantly instigating a fight with each other. It often got to the point where we would start wrestling, punching, and kicking. Holes were put in the drywall and visits to the doctor were as frequent as visits to the grocery store. Over time, she learned to become a great mediator.

On top of her love, kindness, and the thousands of hours she spent with me making my school lunch, playing fake doctor, watching *Dragon Tales* on VHS, and even giving me an oatmeal bath when I had chickenpox, Isabel helped raise me for the next 12 years of my life, and over time, became my *Second Mother*.

So when Adam offered a free ticket to fly to Oaxaca to visit her, I took it in a heartbeat.

As we entered the rustic village, wall enclosures separated the houses. Some were still made of the same mud of Isabel's childhood home, while others had been upgraded to more sturdy materials, like cement and brick.

We took a turn into a narrow street and parked in front of her home. We were immediately greeted by a 15-foot tall blue steel gate that even Hannibal's elephants couldn't break into. I wondered why Isabel needed extra security.

"Oh Sammy, 'dis gate is never locked. I even have a smaller one next to it!" she said, as if she could read my mind.

She pointed to the smaller doorway gate with an unlocked latch, directly adjacent to the blue behemoth.

After Isabel spent many years raising me and Adam in Washington, she continued to work a few more years in Los Angeles with a number of other families, but eventually decided to move back home to take care of her 90-year-old father. When she returned, she bought land in Villa Díaz Ordaz, around the house her father had built out of concrete. Isabel moved back in and transformed her father's house into a place of beauty.

We entered through the blue behemoth to a large circular dirt lawn surrounded by a wall of brick that eventually connected back to the main gate. She had enough fully-grown flowers to make a small garden, some coming from the dirt lawn, and others neatly placed in pots around the circular lawn.

Flowers weren't the only kind of plant that Isabel was fond of. She also grew a small farm filled with plants bearing bell peppers, corn, and lettuce. As we were walking around the dirt lawn, she pointed out a large pile of recently harvested corn that was sitting on a slab of concrete.

The distant sound of a gobble startled me, until we realized that Isabel wasn't only into horticulture. She caged off half a dozen turkeys and chickens in her front yard that provided her with fresh meat and eggs. The chickens lived in a small enclosure in the back corner of the house, next to all her gardening and lawn equipment. It was a small shed with a thin roof and no door. The turkeys were wrapped in a large wire fence enclosure that only took up a quarter of the lawn space. They frequently gobbled in 30-minute intervals unless you decided to speak to one of them, and then they would all gobble back in unison.

The house itself, which was lined with cement and brick, didn't look to be built only as a place to sleep. The outside was meticulously designed. A row of bricks was used as the trim around the two large open windows in front of the house where they eventually intersected at the front door, making a beautiful zipper pattern. Inside the house, the walls, floor, and ceiling were lined with concrete.

Isabel wasn't fond of unnecessary luxuries— only enough to live a comfortable life. Entering the house, the main room was mostly barren. There was a large wooden picnic-style table, one rocking chair, and a small welcome mat to wipe your feet on. That was it.

We were also greeted by Isabel's father, who was quite frail at the age of 90. His skin was wrinkled like leather and most of his teeth were missing, but I could see the excitement on his face when he saw us come through the door. Taking turns, Adam and I both gently held his frail hands in ours, like a delicate handshake.

He had only heard about us through the stories that Isabel brought back. This was the first time he could feel our faces instead of just looking at them in photographs. He started speaking to Isabel. He was so soft-spoken. You could see the amount of energy it took for him to muster a complete sentence for Isabel to translate to us.

"He says that he never expect you guys to come here!"

He smiled and took slow and cautious steps back to his room, telling us that he was to take his daytime nap.

Isabel showed us to our room through a large metal door that had to be lifted up, then pushed open. There were two beds— one the size of a standard twin and the other short enough for either of our feet to dangle off the end. Like siblings, we fought over who got which bed since neither of us wanted the smaller one.

Siblings are like the worst acupuncturists, since they know all your pain points and know how to press on them to get under your skin. Eventually, we struck a deal to trade off each night, but in retrospect, I should have given the larger bed to him. After all, *he paid for my plane ticket.*

The room was almost barren. The walls and floors were also lined with cement, so your feet would get cold if you weren't wearing socks. On the opposite side of the room, there was a hanging box with pictures and flowers like a miniature *ofrenda*. It was a shrine for Isabel's mother who had passed away. I decided to not go near it.

By the time we got settled in, it was 11 o'clock at night, so we decided to rest for the full day we had in store for us.

Another night in a monotonous life.

DAY 2

I woke up at five in the morning after tossing and turning all night. I pressed the palms of my hands over my temple. The jingle started again.

Another monotonous day in a monoto—

No. Bury that thought in the dirt. Try to enjoy the day.

I buried my head back into the pillow, but I couldn't fall back asleep. I laid in bed for another two hours before getting up. There was no mucus in the back of my throat, and Adam was still snoring like a lumberjack. I entered the main room to the smell of poached eggs and the crisp burning of wheat. Isabel already had breakfast going, flipping the bright yellow yolk in the frying pan.

"'Dees eggs are from the chickens. The more fresh you can get, the better they is!"

She put a white porcelain plate down in front me, two scrambled eggs (without cheese), and a piece of bread.

Dear Lord, she was right. They were some of the best eggs I had ever had. I stuffed them into my face like I was in a pie-eating contest. She put a plate down for Adam for when he would wake up and sat at the table with me.

I asked for a glass of water, but Isabel declined and offered something better. "Sammy," she said, putting her hand on my shoulder. "Let me make you homemade hot chocolate."

She went into the kitchen and brought out a small green vase with cocoa extract inside. She took a wooden spoon, placed it in the vase, and whipped the spoon back and forth by rubbing the palms of her hands together with the spoon lodged in between. She served me the hot chocolate with a side of authentic Oaxacan bread called *pan de cazuela.* The bread was warm and moist, sugary and fluffy like biting into a baked cloud coated in sugar cane.

I'm bringing this back home, I thought to myself.

I looked outside and saw Isabel's father near the plants in her garden. He wore a faded grey sweater with a striped collared shirt underneath, and baggy blue jeans. He stood motionless for a bit until he bent down and tugged one of the plants from the ground. Isabel noticed and shook her head while pouring herself a glass of water.

"When I leave 'dees house, he always pulls my plants out of the ground. It drives me nuts!" She took a big gulp of water from a green plastic cup. "Even sometimes when I am here, he still gets up so early and picks these plants."

Some 30 minutes later, Adam sluggishly entered the main room, still half-asleep, and devoured his breakfast. His eyes lit up as well when the eggs hit his tongue.

Lupita and Tony came over for breakfast as well. Their five-seater Volkswagen sedan was waiting for us on the other side of the blue behemoth. Isabel didn't listen to my concerns about long and arduous activities as she laid out the plan for the day.

Monte Albán was our first stop, then we'd go into town for authentic Oaxacan food, and after that, we'd visit Santa María del Tule to see the Árbol del Tule— one of the largest trees in Oaxaca.

When breakfast wrapped up, Adam went to brush his teeth, Lupita and Tony finished their coffee, and Isabel tended to the dishes in the kitchen. I followed her, asking if she needed any help, but like the generous and kind woman she always was, she declined my offer.

I was about to turn my head and leave when her fridge caught my eye. It was decorated in old family photos. Some were of Isabel's nieces and nephews, some of herself, and some of me and Adam when we still couldn't chew solid foods. Isabel noticed my attention to the fridge and walked over.

"I love 'dees ones so much. You and Adam were 'jas babies."

What was beautiful about some of these photos was that I had never seen any of them at my *own* house growing up. These were all new to me. New images of *myself.*

"This is unbelievable," I told her. "I've never seen any of these photos before."

"These here on my fridge are my special ones," she jubilantly said. There was an interesting pattern among the photos. Adam was either whining or had his mouth open, smiling an enormous smile. I, on the other hand, was evidently more reserved and quiet. My mouth was rarely open, and if it was, I was usually giving a timid smile.

"You were so quiet!" Isabel added, as if reading my mind again. "Was so hard to get you to do a big smile."

I laughed and nodded my head in agreement.

"I was just always thinking, I guess," I said.

She nodded in agreement. "You was always thinking. Even when nobody thinks you was paying attention, you were!"

I smiled and turned to her. "Remember the bad word story?"

Of course she did. Her eyes lit up as she put her hand over her chest and chuckled to herself.

"Sammy, I never forget this one!"

Adam and I were around five and seven years old at the time. Isabel was doing something in the kitchen until she stubbed her toe and yelled out a four-letter expletive. According to Isabel, I was playing with my toys, completely unaware of what had happened, so I ignored what she said. But Adam couldn't.

"I remember he begged me so much to say this one again!" Isabel remarked. She pantomimed Adam putting his hands together in a praying gesture. *"Oh, please, Isabel! Please say this word one more time. It will make me so happy!"*

I ignored Adam's begging and tended to my toys while Isabel refused to repeat the word. Adam couldn't let that go so over the next couple of days, he kept begging Isabel every day to repeat the word. (*"Oh, please, Isabel! Just one time. I want to know this word!"*) She never caved, but I got sick of his whining.

"Nobody even knew you were paying attention to this one," Isabel said. "One day, you turn to Adam and you say, '*You really want to know the word?*' and you say the word so perfectly! Adam was so shocked and he thank you. He was so happy!"

It was a hilarious story. One that bolstered my quietude, as well as my observance of things around me. We both laughed and continued to look at the other photos tacked onto the fridge. Isabel pointed to one photo that was held up by a magnet of the United States Capitol building.

"'Dees one here is my favorite!"

She plucked it off the fridge and handed it to me. '*25 4 '95'* was written in orange analog text in the top right corner. *1995*. It was a picture from when my age was still counted in months rather than years.

I was wearing a baby blue onesie patterned with colorful ropes and yellow stars. Isabel sat on her knees with my head resting in her arms. Adam was lying on his back, wearing nothing but a diaper with his tiny legs propped in the air toward Isabel. The icing on the cake was the expression on Isabel's face. She looked directly into the camera and gave a "what have I gotten myself into" face in a playful way.

But on top of all that, the bright red cherry on top of the cake, sitting delicately on top of the icing: *a rare, jubilant smile across my face.*

I instantly knew why this picture was her favorite.

After everyone finished their breakfast and brushed their teeth, we all crammed into the Volkswagen sedan and headed out of the village to our first destination— Monte Albán. As a hotspot for tourists visiting Oaxaca, Monte Albán was the site of ancient Zapotec ruins and temples built over 1500 years ago. The ruins looked similar to the ziggurats built in ancient Mesopotamia, and the only reason I knew this was because I had to build one as a diorama when I was in sixth grade.

"Have you been here before?" I asked Isabel. She was wearing a blue jean jacket, dark pants, and a green floppy sun hat that blocked her entire head if you were looking down at her.

"I never been to this one," she said. "This is my first time. It's so far from me!" Monte Albán was 40 minutes away from the village. Then again, Isabel didn't have a car and no reason to come here. She rarely left the village, for everything she needed was right there: her friends, family, *her turkey and chickens.*

On the way to our next destination, we stopped at a small pizza shop to quell Adam's appetite. I lost mine on the car ride over.

"I need to find some authentic Oaxacan food," he declared in the car. Isabel smiled and started giving directions to Tony in Spanish.

"Don't you worry, I know a place!" she patted Adam's kneecap. We were all sitting in the same arrangement as yesterday. Isabel in the middle, me on the right, and Adam on the left, with Tony driving and Lupita riding shotgun.

They had small conversations in Spanish to themselves and occasionally with Isabel for directions. A yellow truck with a red bar enclosure sitting on top of the flatbed pulled up next to us, holding six cattle all in different shades of black, brown, and white.

"Are you hungry, Sammy?" Isabel asked. I glanced away from looking at the truck as it took a left turn away from us.

"No, I'm fine!" *Fabricated enthusiasm.* "I'm weirdly not hungry right now, so I can wait 'till dinner."

Isabel never took an answer like that at face value. Growing up, she would take me and Adam on walks to the park. When we were in Los Angeles visiting my dad, we would hop on the Big Blue Bus and ride to a nearby swing set or jungle gym. Her fanny pack was always filled with baby carrots (which I hated), trail mix (which I was neutral about), and PB&J sandwiches with the crusts cut off (which I loved).

She would ask if I was hungry and if I wasn't, she would tell me that I needed to eat. "You need to grow, Sammy." She would then empty a few baby carrots from the baggie into her hand and offer them to me.

"Take this much and eat them." I always obliged.

But I was an adult now. I was old enough to buy my own food, open a Roth IRA, or join a traveling circus. Isabel smiled at my response and rubbed her hand on my back.

"You don't need more food. You so big already!"

I started twirling my hair, knotting the strands together, and pulling them out. Adam reached over Isabel and smacked my head.

"Cut that shit out," he ordered. I gave him an '*okay my bad*' face. He twirled his hair too. Not as much as me, but he was the only one who really kept the habit in check.

"You gotta stop doing that," he added.

I know, I know.

The four of us watched Adam wolf down about eight slices of authentic Oaxacan pizza— assembled with tomatoes, avocados, string cheese, hearty beef, and a sort of brown paste that I wasn't sure about. But the scent was wonderful. Now I was hungry.

We then drove to the town center of Santa María del Tule to see the Árbol del Tule— a beautiful tree with an incredibly thick trunk. The town plaza was full of families, since a small carnival was taking place simultaneously. We walked through the small shops similar to a bazaar with souvenirs, knick-knacks, and jewelry. Isabel was my designated translator. If I was interested in buying something, I would ask her how much it was, and she would relay the shopkeeper's answer.

"If you want something, you come find me!" she said. "These shops, they make you pay more if you American."

Nothing stood out to any of us, so we made the journey back to Isabel's village.

Lupita and Tony dropped us off at the house to see Isabel's father sitting outside. Isabel noticed that he pulled some of the flowers out of the ground while we were gone, as he always did. Isabel ignored this, as she was seemingly used to his behavior and started to make dinner. She wanted to show us how she made homemade tortillas, so she guided us outside and over to where the chickens were kept.

Next to the enclosure, there was a door that neither of us noticed before. Inside, Isabel had a small kitchen lined with brick walls. But this kitchen didn't have a stove, refrigerator, or sink. It was much different. She had what looked like a green stool, but it wasn't for sitting; it was a tall tortilla press. She placed a ball of kneaded bread onto the top of the stool and pressed down on a lever to flatten the bread.

"No way our Mother will come and do this," Adam jokingly asserted. Isabel laughed.

"Tell Mommy if she come, she will do this one!" Isabel challenged with a grunt as she pressed down on the tortilla press.

She had a cement ring with a plastic cover on top. Sticks and branches were sticking out from under the cement ring, which Isabel used for kindling. She lit the branches under the cement ring and placed the tortillas on top of the plastic cover for them to cook. The chickens gobbled outside and Adam video-called our mother, father, aunt, uncle, and grandparents to showcase Isabel making food the hard way. All of them were amazed, as was I.

"I make it special for the boys!" Isabel told my dad when he was up to bat on the video call. Adam was holding the phone over the cement ring, watching the tortillas cook under the kindling fire.

"Adam!" my dad's digital voice blared through the phone. "You're getting the Taj Mahal treatment there!"

Adam cackled. "Why don't you get your fat *culo* over here and Isabel can make you the fresh tortillas!"

He cackled too— a static, electronic cackle.

"Sammy," my Dad's voice muffled over the telephone wires. "How is it? Are you enjoying yourself?"

"It's unbelievable," I replied. And it really was.

The night ended with good food and a beautiful starry sky. I got ready for bed, took a hot shower, and began brushing my teeth. Adam entered the bathroom just to put his finger in my ear. I swatted at him and he scurried away like a flustered raccoon.

As I was about to lay in bed, the thoughts started to creep inside my head again.

Who am I? Why am I so—. Stop it. I mentally bludgeoned the thoughts again and focused on Oaxaca, the fresh scrambled eggs, the bustled souvenir shops flooded with people enjoying the weekend, Monte Albán, the *pan de cazuel*, and everything else in between.

Slowly but surely, I drifted to sleep.

DAY 3

After three days of forgetting my razor at home, a small patch of stubble started to grow on my face. I entered the kitchen for breakfast and Isabel fixed her sight on my scruffy stubble.

"When you don't have nathin', you look so young!"

Isabel looked elated and tended back to moving the yellow yolk of the fresh eggs around the pan with a wooden paddle.

"So handsome, anyway!"

Our last full day was jam-packed, so we got going quickly. Adam wolfed down his eggs again, and Lupita and Tony were there waiting to pick us up.

We visited San Pablo Villa de Mitla to look at more shops. Then, we drove to the Museo Comunitario Balaa Xtee Guech Gulal, a museum where they had replicas of early Oaxacan houses, similar to the mud and stick one that Isabel grew up in.

After the museum, we stopped by a shop that hand-made carpets and rugs with a giant wood-weaving loom. What was most astounding was the fact that Isabel went over to the weaving loom and started using it without any direction or questions.

"I remember I use 'dees one so much," Isabel said. "I would make scarfs, blankets, and rugs all the time!"

She had a long nostalgic look in her eyes, as if using the weaving loom rekindled fond memories from years ago. We then stopped at a *mezcal* factory (on Adam's insistence) and picked up a few souvenir bottles. The day ended with us driving back to the village and spending some time in the town square before dusk. Inside, there was a police station with officers sitting outside, chatting in Spanish to one another.

A group of kids were playing with dolls and action figures on the sidewalk while their parents mingled with each other. It was such a small but vibrant village with an enormous church serving as its centerpiece. We went inside to see the podium beautifully decorated with flowers, candles, and Christian mosaics framed in gold.

Dusk came quickly, but before we closed our final night in Oaxaca, Isabel walked us through the *pueblo* to visit one of her sisters.

As we walked around, police cars patrolled the streets to ensure the safety and security of the village.

"The new mayor," Isabel exclaimed, referencing the police cars, "is the one who put these 'tings in place. We never had 'dees one before."

We kept walking through the dimly lit *pueblo*. We saw a group of kids playing jacks under a streetlight, since the entire *pueblo* was near pitch black at night from the lack of lights. We met up with Isabel's sister, who was overflowing with affection for me and Adam. We talked for an hour, learning about their lives growing up in Villa Díaz Ordaz. Adam did most of the talking, while I stayed quiet as usual. As it got late, we eventually said our goodbyes and walked back to the house.

The night came to a close as Adam and I both packed up our suitcases to get ready to leave the following afternoon. It was a great trip. I got to see Isabel, visit some beautiful places in Oaxaca, and learn a bit about its history.

I was feeling great. I even barged in the bathroom to stick my finger in Adam's ear while he was brushing his teeth. I gave Isabel a hug, told her I would see her in the morning, and walked back into my room to get ready for bed. I curled under a thick crochet blanket and stared up at the grey cement ceiling. Adam came in a few moments later and shut off the lights.

Now I was staring at sheer darkness. As I drifted to sleep, I thought about tomorrow. I thought about saying goodbye to Isabel and boarding the small carrier plane. I thought about Martin waiting to pick me up from the airport with fresh tire marks on the concrete. I would then get to my apartment, unlock the door, walk back into my room, and then, *nothing*.

Everything would still be there, and nothing would have changed. Then, the flurry of thoughts rushed in: *Is this what you want? Is this who you are? Where are your friends? Where is your community? What do you believe in? Are you happy? Fulfilled? Is this a good life? Is this the life you want to live?*

And then: *Who am I? Why am I so alone? What do I believe?*

And finally, as expected: *Another monotonous night in a rather monotonous life.*

I let the thoughts fill my head. I didn't even make a half-hearted attempt to swat them away. I let them fill my head, pushing into every crack and crevice they could find. I tossed back and forth in my bed for what felt like an hour.

At some point in the night, I closed my eyes and drifted into what felt like sleep, only to be woken up again.

Chapter 3

I opened my eyes. I couldn't remember the time, but I woke up halfway into the night. Something had woken me up, but I didn't know what.

The air felt light, and that pernicious thought of returning to the states, everything unchanged, bubbled to the surface.

Going back home without some form of peace or enlightenment. Going back without any answers. My skin began to crawl. The hairs on my arms standing straight up.

I got up and pressed my bare feet onto the cold cement floor. I looked over to see Adam still snoring like a cursed banshee. I didn't know what to do, so I began pacing back and forth, examining every single detail in the room.

The finish on the old makeup table, the pile of VHS tapes in front of the small CRT television, the color of the flowers resting on the shrine of Isabel's mother. I entered the kitchen to get myself a cup of water. I lifted and pushed out the heavy metal door gently, as to not make a sound and wake anyone.

As the door opened, moonlight pierced through the large windows of the dark and barren main room. I stopped in place. "Barren" may not have been the right adjective to use. I stammered, standing frozen in place.

I felt as if something inside of me came to life– abruptly and out of nowhere. I wasn't sure what to say.

I assumed Isabel would make the first gesture, but she remained silent. She sat on one side of the wooden bench, stirring her homemade cocoa with a wooden spoon. I felt a sense of stillness with her. She radiated the same kindness and affection that she always did, but was holding herself more formally. Her back was arched up against the wall and her hands were clasped around a small cup.

She noticed my entrance as she took the spoon out of the cup and sipped her homemade cocoa. She flashed a vibrant smile at me. I knew I would have to start the conversation.

"Why are you still awake?" I asked.

She took another long sip of her homemade cocoa and gathered herself. She drew a smile and arched her back to respond.

"Sammy," she said. "I woke up at precisely the same time as you. I'm awake because you're awake."

She was different. She spoke in fluent and proper English, and yet her Oaxacan accent didn't falter. Her tone was just as soft and warming, but her speech was sharp and more precise. Her friendliness was unmatched by her stillness and equanimity. She raised her cup of hot cocoa toward me.

"Would you like a sip?" she asked. "You know I make it homemade."

I was still in some form of paralysis, trying to understand her with this new tone of voice. I couldn't ignore the small idiosyncrasy.

"What happened to your voice?" I asked her.

She took a long sip of her cocoa. "My voice has always been like this," she calmly replied.

I started to antagonize her. "No, it hasn't. Why does your voice sound completely different?"

She remained silent. I slowly approached her to get a better look. She looked the same as she did yesterday. I started to rationalize theories in my head.

"It's late, Isabel," I told her. "You shouldn't be awake, you need to get rest. We have a long day tomorrow. Your voice is probably drained from the weekend."

Some of the hot cocoa smeared on the right side of her lip. She wiped it away with her hand.

"It's less important to worry about why I'm awake, Sammy." She put the cup down on top of a brown coaster. "What's more important is why *you're* awake."

What does she mean about me being awake?

Isabel doesn't speak in riddles like an elusive Batman villain. Isabel doesn't speak in a sharp and proper English dialect. Isabel gives bear hugs, packs baggies of carrots and crustless PB&Js, and jubilantly mispronounces words with enthusiasm. This Isabel was different.

A Faux Isabel.

"You're not Isabel," I said to her with conviction.

She smiled. "You'd be right, Sammy," she said in a lively tone. "But I also am. I'm *your* Isabel."

More riddles and more sharpness in her speech.

"What does that even mean?" I asked.

She radiated a smile. "Do you trust me, Sammy?"

I hesitated. "I'm... I'm not sure. This is all so confusing."

"I think you should. You're not awake right now by coincidence. There's a reason. A troubling one."

It seemed pretty obvious as to why anyone would be awake at such an ungodly hour in the night, but I wasn't sure if *Faux Isabel* knew. I'd rather just lie by omission.

"I can't sleep," I told her.

She paused and fixed a face that expressed an insufficient response to the question. I had a feeling she could tell that I gave her a surface layer answer.

"I know why you're awake, Sammy, but I want *you* to tell me. It's important to start with honesty."

I gave her a hesitant stare without an answer. She prodded me.

"Take a breath and relax."

My body was numb and the goosebumps on my arms continued to bevel and grow more defined.

Should I trust her? Faux Isabel was patient. I took a deep breath and mustered a reply.

"I— I've been having thoughts," I stammered like a child.

"What kind of thoughts?"

"Just thoughts."

Isabel frowned. "It's hard to help you if you don't tell me."

"I don't need any help."

Isabel looked at me, my face visibly disheveled, dark and heavy circles around my eyes, with missing gaps of hair in my head.

"I think you do," she calmly stated. I looked down and pressed my feet deeper into the cold cement floor. Vulnerability was not my strong suit. I continuously shrouded my feelings from friends and family to not seem weak or feeble, but this *Faux Isabel* intuitively knew that I wasn't living my best life.

We were in silence until she said, "You can drop the *faux* now," with a bright smile. "It'll be better for the both of us going forward."

I don't think she was limited to the six senses. She took another sip as I lifted an eyebrow and then deflated my skepticism.

Things were funky. I'm in pain and I have unanswered questions. Nothing has seemed to work so far, and I was positive that this wouldn't, either. Best to drop the small idiosyncrasies moving forward.

"I'd hope you wouldn't evade a question you know the answer to, Sammy," Isabel insisted.

I told her I was almost there, but I wasn't. Not even close. We both sat in silence for a moment. I dug my hands into the pockets of my sweatpants to warm them up. I dipped my head down to stare at the cement floor. Isabel didn't want to spell it out, but like a deaf contestant at a National Spelling Bee, she felt like she had to, since I clearly couldn't hear what she was saying.

"Sammy," she said. "There are things about yourself that you believe to be *fundamentally flawed*. There are pains in your life you have been dealing with for a long time. Questions that have remained unanswered. Am I right?"

I looked back at her, staring into her marble eyes. "Yeah, that's right," I said as I took my hands out of my pockets and fixed my slouched posture.

Isabel smiled. "And you've known about these aspects about yourself for quite some time."

I nodded. Isabel flashed another smile and took a sip of her hot cocoa. "So, I want to ask you again, Sammy. *Why are you awake?*"

I fell silent for a moment and thought of mustering a better answer.

"Because I want to leave these pains," I said. "The uncertainty I have about myself as a person, the isolation I've felt for many years, the inauthenticity of my beliefs and values."

Isabel palmed her hands together. She let out a deep and meditative hum as she arched her back against the cement wall.

"Your pains need to be addressed, Sammy."

No shit. They needed to be fixed years ago. I've been driving a rusty, dilapidated pick-up truck in desperate need of an overdue repair. Isabel sensed that I said something crass, for her mouth almost opened to say something. However, it closed before the words came out. In lightspeed, she went from expressionless to ebullient.

"But how can I fix my pains without understanding how to answer the questions swirling inside my head?" I said, while finger-circling my ear. "I've been struggling with developing myself into a happy and fulfilled person for too long. I'm awake because I don't know how to fix my pains."

Isabel's expressionless face came back, but she kept her calm and soothing aura. She sighed and painted a smile on her face.

"You shouldn't fix these parts about your life, because some of them may not need fixing."

"Um, okay. Then— then what should I do?"

She picked up the wooden spoon and gently stirred the hot cocoa in her cup. "*You should simply start to understand them.*"

She removed the spoon and took another long sip of cocoa. More ominous and vague messages like she was this enlightened soothsayer destined to guide me through some hackneyed and overdone hero's journey. *Give me my shield and point me to the damsel in distress already!*

"So how do I understand my pains?" I asked.

Isabel took another sip and smiled.

"A pendulum only swings when it's provoked. A ripple in the water only forms when the lake is disturbed."

More riddles and more vagueness. *The soothsayer has spoken!* I flexed an eyebrow at her, curious as to where she would go with this.

She smiled at my perplexed facial expression. When Isabel smiled, she never showed her teeth, but just a flexed lip and beveled cheeks.

"Progress and understanding don't come without action," she said. "They need a certain force to remove the inertia. You're awake because you don't know how to *address* these pains. They still need to be opened up. Do you want to open up these pains, Sammy?"

The soothsayer did something I didn't think it would do— *hit a pain point.* I immediately thought of the torment my mind put itself through.

I tried to do everything on my own. I never asked for help. I hadn't been at peace with myself for a long time. At this point, I might as well take any offer of insight I could.

"I do," I replied softly, accepting like I was standing at the altar. "I want to open up these pains."

Isabel sat back against the wall and smiled.

"Then we have a lot to talk about."

Chapter 4

THE BOX

Isabel asked me to sit across from her at the table. My heroic and spiritual journey didn't start with me crossing a cavern of ungodly danger or fighting a mythical hydra whose heads grow back after they're chopped off.

It started with taking three steps, barefoot on a cold cement floor, to sit at a wooden table with no back support. *How dangerous.*

I have terrible posture. I can't sit up straight without leaning up against something for more than five minutes before my back starts to ache. But when I sat down at the bench with no back support and continued to sit in silence while Isabel meditatively hummed to herself for what felt like forever, I didn't feel pain at all.

She finally opened her eyes, exhaled, and smiled.

"What was that all about?" I prodded.

She stayed radiant and ignored my question by asking another. "Have you made any attempts to understand your pain, Sammy?"

Truth is, I had done a ton of crap. Tried to get out more. Tried to see more friends and act like I was interested in what they were doing in their lives. I read lots of self-improvement books. Tried to forge my own path. Focused on a passion.

Yes, a passion. That's what I need. Find a wife, eat more asparagus, and for God's sake, do at least one pushup a day. I've reflected. Written, I mean *journaled*, about my past.

Wait. I paused. *My Journal.*

"I've been keeping a journal," I told her.

Her ears perked up. "A journal about what?"

"About past events in my life. I write every Sunday."

I didn't add that I would sit in nearly pitch black darkness, breathe terrible air, and strain my eyes all for the glory of journaling.

Isabel looked intrigued. "And has that helped?"

"Not really," I replied, seeming deflated.

"Have you come to understand anything about yourself?"

"No."

"Not anything?"

I shook my head. "Nada."

She hummed, and I could hear the vibrations coming from her mouth. She sat up straight and smiled, as always, with a soothing aura.

"Well, that makes sense."

I gave her a puzzled look. "What do you mean?"

"Your journal. It hasn't worked."

"Yeah, but how does that make sense?"

She smiled. "It hasn't worked because you're hesitant."

Isabel pulled out a wooden chest from under the table, seemingly out of nowhere, like it was sitting by her side the whole time out of sight, waiting to be revealed at the right moment. It was coated with a brown finish and was relatively small— similar in size to a tissue box.

The chest had three latches, two of which were straps, and one with a copper swivel latch in the middle of the two straps— representing three different locks— all of them tightly shut. She placed the chest on the table between us.

"Why do you think I'm showing this to you, Sammy?"

Again, I looked just as confused when I was slouching with my hands buried into my pockets.

"I don't know," I shrugged. "I assume you're gonna tell me anyway."

I kept some skepticism in the back of my head. Isabel hit a pain point, but I had the expectation that this would go down in flames like a *Led Zeppelin*.

Isabel raised an eyebrow at me. She must have seen that I was still unsure about all this. She picked up the chest.

"This chest holds your pains, the ones you've known for quite some time now. The aspects of your life that you are so desperately trying to understand."

"I guess," I shrugged again in unenthusiastic agreement. Again, Isabel raised a kind eyebrow at me.

"Conviction is important, Sammy, but not for right now."

"Okay, so what's the point of the box?"

Isabel smiled and clutched the box to her chest. She then displayed it out to me for my examination.

"Inside this box are your pains, and the locks represent your hesitations."

"My hesitations?"

"The premonitions and feelings about what will happen when you eventually remove the locks on this box and the contents inside are revealed to everyone."

My bottom lip quivered as I felt a quiet riot brew inside my head. Pain is as common as a tree, rock, or a puddle of water, but I couldn't find my own. Now, I saw a physical representation of this stubborn boulder blocking the entrance into the place where I could finally answer those unanswered questions.

"Do you know what's inside?" Isabel asked.

"I . . . I don't know," I stammered.

"No?"

"I don't know what's inside." I also knew I didn't have the strength to move the boulder.

Isabel smiled. "But you do know. You already know what's inside the box, because they're *your* pains. You already put them in there. To make any sort of progress, the locks need to be removed."

"So, what should we do?"

"So, what should *you* do?" Isabel corrected.

I gave her a feeble smile. Isabel was giving me personal agency. She flashed a kind smile back and glanced at the three latches.

"Let's start addressing these locks."

THE FIRST LOCK

Isabel glanced at my outfit. A Fruit of the Loom t-shirt with a loose collar, baggy sweatpants, and a pair of flip-flops I've had since attending Jewish summer camp when I was 14. Not exactly the type of outfit Vera Wang would put on a storefront mannequin.

"You're frugal, Sammy," she stated. "Like me!"

She wasn't wrong. I'm already an incredibly cheap person, which is bad news for any gold-diggers who'll just find Pyrite after dating me for a couple months, but good news for my bank account.

"This is what I wear to bed," I said, defending my terrible fashion choices. "I have nicer clothes."

"I didn't make that claim by looking at your outfit from head to toe. I know you have nicer clothes back home. But the one thing I do know is that you're cheap."

"And what does that have to do with unlocking the box?"

Isabel flashed a smile. "You grew up wealthy, is that true?"

I couldn't push her back on this. I did grow up wealthy, and I was humbled and grateful for it every day. I'm not talking "wealthy" like mansions, yachts, and family vacations to the Maldives, but I'm fortunate enough to not know what it's like to live paycheck to paycheck, to work two or three jobs to keep a roof above my head, and to not have access to healthcare within arms-reach. These are privileges I inherited from living in a stable household.

It was an output of my father, who grew up with little means and pursued a lucrative career in medicine, while my mother sacrificed her career to raise Adam and I, alleviating our childhood from any of the sufferings they had to go through.

"I'm fortunate for all the help I received," I replied. "I don't know how much more thankful I can be."

Isabel nodded. "Do you think your life is better because of all that help?"

"Of course it is," I replied instinctively. It was my first statement of conviction. Isabel looked somewhat pleased. At least I didn't stutter like I'd swallowed my tongue.

"Why do you say that, Sammy?" she asked.

"If my life was a ship, then it was already built and waiting for me at the harbor. I'd just have to adjust the sails, turn the wheel, and pick the direction I wanted to go in."

"You think everything was given to you?"

"Absolutely."

A short silence fell over the room. "In my opinion," I added. "I'd have to be a colossal shithead to not even reach the docks."

Isabel nodded again. I had a pernicious feeling that I was setting up her point.

"But growing up wealthy," she added. ". . . isn't all sunshine and rainbows for everyone. It has its drawbacks as well, right?"

"I mean, sure. I guess growing up wealthy somewhat came with a lack of incentive to work hard. People could also take advantage of me. But I don't think it's valuable if I sit here and try to read you a sob story from a book with a golden binding."

Isabel nodded yet again. "Your last statement is proving my point." My pernicious feeling confirmed.

"What do you mean?" I asked.

"What I mean is that you don't believe you're allowed to have problems. You constantly look at all the things that were given to you and try to rationalize to yourself that there's no way you could be suffering."

Isabel wasn't wrong. One 360° spin to see everything in my life was a way for me to invalidate the honest feelings that I was having. I'm financially stable, I have two loving and supportive parents, I'm well-educated, and have a great occupation.

How the hell am I in pain?

"But what does this have to do with me being cheap?"

Isabel radiated a smile. "You feel like you don't deserve to have nice things because they were already given to you, whether, using your own words, *you asked for them or not.*"

"I see that, Isabel. But I do have nice things. Things that I've inherited growing up and things I've earned myself. I'm quite content with what I have. I just choose not to spend money on frivolous stuff."

Isabel hummed to herself. "This doesn't only apply to the physical world— it also applies to the psychological one, too. The abundances you grew up with were frequently used as crutches to try and squash feelings of sadness and pain."

Never have I thought about my physical luxuries as roadblocks in accepting that there were mental luxuries I lacked.

"So, what are you saying?"

Isabel beamed with happiness and clasped the box with her hands. "The first lock," she instructed while pointing to the strap latch on the left side, "that's keeping you from opening it is your wealth—*your upbringing.*"

I was still perplexed at her conclusion. My mouth hung open like Edvard Munch's *The Scream* composition. I had a feeling Isabel could see the shock on my face.

She emphasized her point to me. "Answer this question for me, Sammy. If a man jumps off a two-story building, does he feel the pain of the cement making contact with his legs?" I raised an eyebrow at her, wondering whether this was a trick question or not.

"I think our understanding of anatomy, pain receptors, and the laws of gravity say yes," I replied.

Isabel smiled, but didn't seem so interested in my joke. Sometimes my over-rationalization of things blinded me to their fundamental message. I made a note to myself to only say jokes to myself moving forward.

"My Sammy, I'm not asking if science understands, *I'm asking if you understand.*"

"Yes, I do."

Isabel hummed and nodded. "Now take another man, but this man was raised and bathed in luxury his entire childhood. When he jumps off the same building, does he feel the pain of the cement making contact with his legs?"

"Of course he does."

Isabel looked pleased. "Good. Now take that first man again, when the love of his life leaves him for another partner. Does he feel heartbreak?"

"I suppose so."

"Now take that second man, who was raised and bathed in luxury his entire childhood, when the love of his life leaves him for another partner. Does he also feel heartbreak?"

"I guess so."

"Now, Sammy, if you, who was raised and bathed in a similar form of luxury, had the love of your life leave you for another partner, would you feel heartbreak?

"I think I would, but what does this have to do with the box?"

Isabel smiled and re-clutched the box in her hands.

"A crucial step to opening the box is for you to understand more thoroughly that, despite your cherished and privileged upbringing, *you*, like everyone else in the world, can still suffer."

I leaned back and stroked the three-day-old stubble on my chin for a second before responding. "So, I shouldn't let my wealthy upbringing be a barrier to fixing my pains?

Isabel frowned, but kept her calm and warming speech intact. "The barrier isn't in front of fixing your pains, it's in front of truly *understanding* your pains. It's a barrier to unlocking this box."

"Oh, I see," I said with the monotony of a droned-out college student. Isabel lifted up the strap and unlocked the first latch on the box.

"Baby steps, Sammy."

THE SECOND LOCK

The moonlight was still piercing through the window that stretched across the main room. I peered outside to the circular courtyard. The wind rustled through the branches of the trees. I couldn't see past the tall brick wall that surrounded the courtyard, but it felt as if nobody was on the other side.

It was deadly quiet, as if we were the only two people in the whole *pueblo* . . . until I heard a sound that was too faint and distant to decipher. It sounded like someone smacked a gong from one of the mountain peaks.

"Did you hear that?" I asked.

Isabel was in the kitchen, pouring herself a second serving of hot cocoa. "Second offer," she said, holding up the larger container of cocoa, ignoring my question. I shook my head and she sat back down, her hands curled around the cup.

"You shouldn't give so much attention to sounds," she said. "They're distractions."

From what? Isabel didn't seem to care about the dead silence as much as I did. It was almost as if she was used to it. She began to stir the hot cocoa with the wooden spoon, her lips forming a crisp smile.

"How are you feeling right now?" she asked.

I scratched my neck. "Like, right now?"

"Yes, *like* right now," she said, jabbing fun at my emphasized use of the word *like*. I liked it. The soothsayer had a sense of humor.

"I don't know. I— I feel *unpleasant*. I'm trying to minimize uncertainties I have about myself."

She took a hard, vocal sip. *Shhhhlurp.* She set the cup back down on the coffee table, nodded, and flexed her dimples, filling the room with warmth and tranquility. She closed her eyes and hummed to herself like a monk entering into deep meditation.

"*Uncertainty is psychologically unpleasant,*" she stated. The words rolled so smoothly and cleverly off her tongue. She opened her eyes and fixed her gaze back at me.

"And what do you know about yourself?"

"Very little, to say the least." *Gulp.* "There are lots of things about myself I want to address, but I just don't know how."

She picked up the box and stared at the middle latch.

"Do you know the difference between *good* and *meaningful?*"

What the hell does that mean? I didn't give Isabel a verbal answer, but she still smiled and then inquired.

"The pains you are so desperately trying to understand, are they *good* or *meaningful*?"

"Umm . . . I don't know," I muttered with the confidence of a cowardly child. "Those just seem the same."

Isabel smiled and clasped her hands together, resting them on the table. A slice of un-shadowed moonlight covered her hands in a bright white glow.

"I think it would be helpful to differentiate between *good* and *meaningful*. There is a fundamental difference between the two words. *Good*, while still subjective, holds much more objectivity than *meaningful*."

I gave her a blank face. She continued her explanation, unbothered by my expression. "Let's use *a chemistry book* as an example."

"Okay," I said as I laid my elbows on the table.

"A *good* chemistry book may have the proper formulas, structure, citations, and appendices in the back. It can also be well-written and concise to help anyone study the core tenants of chemistry."

"I see."

"But a *meaningful* chemistry book goes beyond the rigid rules and guidelines that we use to classify a *good* chemistry book—sometimes even breaking them. It will rustle the feathers of people who uphold the objectivity of what's good, but will catalyze the fiery passion in people who look for inspiration."

I scratched the three-day-old stubble on my chin again.

"I think I understand."

Isabel smiled. "In essence, a good chemistry book helps someone better understand the field of chemistry, but *a meaningful chemistry book inspires someone to **become** a chemist.*"

The distinction seemed clear to me, but I was still confused by its relevance. It looked as if Isabel noticed my confusion.

"Does that make sense, Sammy?"

"Kinda."

"*Kinda?*"

"Okay, not really."

She momentarily frowned, but then bounced right back to her ebullient aura. "Sammy, where can pain come from?" she asked.

"Umm . . . I mean, from a lot of things. A traumatic event, a sudden death of a loved one, a harsh upbringing. I mean, those are just the ones that came to mind. There's probably a bunch of other examples."

Isabel nodded. "Have you experienced a traumatic event?"

"Not that I can recall." *Or any that my therapist could uncover.*

"Have you experienced the sudden death of a loved one?"

"Fortunately, no, not yet, at least."

Isabel nodded again. "We classify these pains as objective. We don't dismiss the pain of someone who lost their limbs in combat. We don't dismiss the pain of someone who lost their spouse in a tragic accident. We don't dismiss the pain of someone who was raised in an abusive household with little to no means."

"Yes, I see that. These pains are objectively serious."

"But do you think your pains are just as serious?"

"Not really. As I said, I haven't experienced any of the kinds of events you just mentioned."

Isabel furrowed her brow before drawing a kind smile on her face. "It's not a contest to see who has suffered the most. It's to see how much suffering these pains have caused you as an individual, from how you think the world objectively views pain and suffering does not align with how you view your own. Your process of writing this book is holding you back from truly understanding the pains that are *meaningful* to you, because you don't believe they are. You don't think they're *good enough to even talk about.* You acknowledge that they exist, but you treat them as benign compared to how we objectively characterize pain and suffering."

I stroked my chin yet again, the stubble rough against the skin of my fingers.

"Sammy," Isabel continued, "what does this mean for you?"

Silence. I thought for a brief moment before answering.

"So instead of trying to fix the pains that will be objectively accepted by people I don't care about, I should instead fix the meaningful pains that will have the most positive impact on myself."

Isabel hummed. "Your thinking is correct, but remember, we aren't here to fix your pains. We simply want to *understand* them."

"Right, I need to address the pain and suffering that are *meaningful* to myself instead of *good* for others."

Isabel smiled and lifted the strap to unlatch the second lock. Then, she looked at the middle swivel latch— *the third lock.*

"The last one is always the hardest."

THE THIRD LOCK

Isabel paid no attention to me for a few moments. I sat there twiddling my thumbs like a child in overalls wearing a technicolored spinney hat, waiting for his cartoon-sized lollipop. I swallowed hard and jotted a confused look on my face.

"So . . ." I trailed off. "The third lock."

Isabel hummed to herself and stayed in a meditative trance.

"Are we going to open it?" I prodded.

Silence. It seemed like my question went over her head, for what seemed like the 20th time now.

Silence made me uncomfortable. It always gave me an urge to speak or say something, to throw out some sort of sound vibrations into the void. Isabel finally looked up at me and smiled.

"Do you think you have the ability to understand the pains in your life?" she asked.

I paused before responding.

"What does that mean, exactly?"

Isabel held the box in her hand and pointed to each of the latches. I intently followed her point.

"The first lock on this box addressed your upbringing, an inherited characteristic. The second lock on this box addressed how you viewed your problems, benign in nature relative to how we objectively understand pain and suffering. The third lock on this box addresses your aptitude— your ability and expertise to *understand* and potentially *heal* these pains in your life."

Isabel reiterated her question back to me and I sat for a moment in silence. "I . . . I don't know," I stammered. "Do you think I have the ability to fix the pains in my life?"

"Not to fix the pains, Sammy," she corrected. "When we realize whether we're unhappy, sad, depressed, unfulfilled, or void of peace, we tend to look outward instead of inward. We don't believe we have the power to remedy the pains ourselves. There are plenty of external sources that promise people they can be happy, fulfilled, and at peace with themselves. We're too comfortable asking others for help instead of just asking ourselves."

In that brief moment, a troubling memory filled my head.

"I've used those external sources before, Isabel."

She looked at me in interest and told me to elaborate. I vividly remembered using external sources, specifically sources from other people, who proclaimed they had the cures, keys, secrets, and long-lost ancient scriptures from God himself, to fix whatever aspect of your life that you wanted fixed. They'd tell you to perform a certain action, adopt a certain habit, or create a certain mentality, because it was shown to be beneficial to them, with no evidence that *you'd* get the same results. These are the people who offer promises that are far removed from the outcomes.

"Why did you pursue these sources in the first place?" Isabel asked.

"Well, I didn't have personal definitions for myself. I didn't have personal measures of happiness, success, or fulfillment, or anything else."

She reclined her back against the cement wall behind her.

"It's tough to understand your pains when you don't know exactly when you'll actually understand them."

"Right. I spent a lot of time by myself, engrossed in vices that made me comfortable to avoid creating them."

"You craved desire."

"Like everyone else in the world? Yeah, I craved desire. But the desires I was pursuing weren't fulfilling or meaningful."

"So instead of self-reflecting and taking a holistic approach to figure out these important tenants, you consulted external sources."

Exactly, I told her. It started when I made the decision that I was powerless. I started watching self-improvement content online. I had the belief that I didn't have the willpower to fix myself, so I was susceptible to any quick formula or structure of techniques to turn my life in the right direction. I explained this progression to Isabel. She sat back against the wall and let out a meditative hum.

"And what happened after you watched these videos?" she asked.

"Well, I learned different formulas, tactics, and frameworks from different sources. From there, I would just try them out, hoping one would fix my pains. I mean, ingesting knowledge without action is pretty pointless, right?"

Isabel lifted a kind eyebrow at me, but quickly went back into a state of stillness. "Did any of them work?"

"Not really," I said in a deflated tone. "It took me a long time to realize that I kept seeing simple cure-all formulas for overly complex and deeply entrenched problems. These gurus would tout their principles, habits, frameworks, rules, and guidelines, or whatever you wanna call it, as universal antidotes using these– *augh*, what's the word– *vague* and generic phrases that would boost my ego and give me the false impression that I was becoming better. When in reality, I was merely *feeling* better."

Isabel nodded. "But you kept going. You didn't stop."

"Because I assumed that one of them had to work."

Something always has to work. Something always has to fit. The world doesn't leave loose screws lying around. Even the son of God was a carpenter.

"But none of them did," Isabel grimly noted. "Why didn't they work?"

I like visuals. Pictures, graphics, charts, anything visual. My peers in elementary school read the text-heavy *Harry Potter* books while I preferred the superhero comic book, *Captain Underpants.* Funny how my occupation now involves writing code (letters and words) and writing books on the side (way more letters and words).

I asked Isabel for a piece of paper and a pen. She retrieved both from a drawer in the kitchen, a fresh white sheet of 8x11 inch paper, and a black ballpoint pen.

"It's all a *cycle*," I said. "Let's say you're unhappy. Maybe you hate your job, or maybe you're in an awful marriage. It doesn't matter. The point is, you're unhappy. The opposite of happy. Your view of the world is binary— happy or unhappy."

Isabel seemed to be listening with intense interest. Her gaze never broke from my eyes.

"So now you're unhappy. What do you do?" I asked semi-rhetorically. Isabel let out a brief hum and scratched her chin.

"You need to figure out *why* you're so unhappy."

"Right. Maybe you ask your friends or your family. Hell, maybe even your partner, if you have the stones. But most of us don't. Asking people close to us for help makes us vulnerable. We don't like that image."

"So, what do we do instead?"

"We ask others. Others who don't judge us, because they don't know us. Others who can give us a manual, a plan of attack, a roadmap to newfound happiness."

"Where do you find these people?" she asked.

"Oh, anywhere. In books, at conferences, at lectures, and now more than ever, on the internet. There are plenty of them, some of them clear-cut, analytical types with rock-solid credentials and others are just pseudo-experts speaking in verbal Caesar salad."

"I see."

"Then you start reading or viewing their content. A book, or a video, or whatever medium you prefer."

I pushed the ink onto the pen near the top center of the page and wrote 'Ingest External Content.'

"This is the first step," I explained to Isabel. "They give you the framework, the keys, the secrets, or whatever you want to call it."

"You ingest more, because everything they say flows so well. It's just *vague* enough to feel like this person is speaking directly to you."

I wrote 'Surge of Motivation' below and to the right, and drew a line connecting the two phrases.

"Is this what happened to you?" Isabel asked.

"On YouTube specifically. It was like a treasure trove, littered with videos that flaunted irresistible titles that were impossible to avoid. *'Five Easy Steps to Happiness.' 'How to Find Fulfillment in your Life.'* And so on."

"But why even listen to them in the first place?"

"They're viewed as thought leaders who held the same problems, fixed themselves with a special formula, and are now sharing the formula with us so that we may achieve the same outcome."

Isabel gave me a small frown, as if she wasn't pleased with my answer.

"I see . . ." she said, letting those 'e's trail at the end. "So, what comes next?"

With the black ballpoint pen, I wrote 'Take Action' on the page, directly below 'Ingest External Content,' below and to the left of 'Surge of Motivation.' I drew an arrow from 'Surge of Motivation' to 'Take Action.' The lines connecting to each of the phrases created a half-circle.

"You follow it, with action." I smirked. "Ingesting knowledge without action is pretty pointless, right?"

Isabel gave a soft, toothless smile and nodded.

"But your actions don't always have an immediate impact, right? Sometimes you fail. Things don't work out. You lose steam."

I wrote 'Action Fails or Motivation Fades' on the left side, directly in line with 'Surge of Motivation.' I drew a curved arrow from 'Take Action' and connected it to 'Action Fails or Motivation Fades.'

"So now what do you do?" Isabel asked.

"Well, you can keep repeating the action, which will probably get the same result, and Einstein will cast you a displeased frown. Eventually, your motivation will deplete anyway."

"Or?"

"Or . . . you can find a new framework. A new set of principles. A new *anything* that yields new actions. And you get those new principles by simply ingesting more content."

I drew the final curved arrow from 'Action Fails or Motivation Fades' back to the first step, 'Ingest External Content.'

This yielded a fully-drawn cycle on the page: *My Cyclical Dependency.*

Ingest
External
Content

Surge of
Motivation

Take
Action

Action Fails or
Motivation
Fades

"I just couldn't break out of this cycle," I solemnly told Isabel, changing the hypothetical scenario to be about myself. "I was like a pavlovian Golden Retriever. Flash me a shiny chew toy of over-delivered promises of living a better life— one with all my pains fixed— and I'll sink my canines into it immediately."

Isabel nodded and looked attentively at the diagram.

"It just became so . . . so effortless," I added. "I had an urge to find anything that gave me a little kick of motivation, but it always fizzled out. And when it did, I fell back into my bad habits and moved on to find another framework to use. My road to progress and improvement became a Möbius strip. I was reliant on motivation and action toward improvement— a continuous path that didn't have a clear end in sight."

Isabel took a long sip of her cocoa. I completely forgot it was still resting on the table. She put the cup down in the same spot and connected with my eyes. She looked down at the diagram, grabbed the sheet, and folded it four times.

"You should keep this as a reminder," she said, offering me the folded paper. I stuffed it in my pocket.

She hummed and seemed to have gone into deep thought, closing her eyes. This brief moment of silence made me think about Evan Arleno— my psychology professor in college.

I wasn't the most attentive student. I usually dozed off or watched highlights of Kobe plunging daggers from behind the arc while Mr. Arleno rambled about the Stanford prison experiment.

But one of his lessons perked my ears. It was about *Occam's Razor*— the idea that the simplest claim is usually the one that's right. Jokingly, through my path of self-discovery, I referred to it as *Occam's Chisel*, since chisels are a popular tool in both plastic surgery and sculpting— professions that remove unwanted excess to unearth something more attractive.

This knowledge supported the idea that, in order for me to be 'insert superlative here,' I'd need to chisel off certain features about myself. Isabel stopped humming to herself and continued to analyze the situation.

"Sammy," she said in a pleasant tone. "What about your friends and family? Were they able to see this?"

"Not really. To everyone around me, it looked like I was making progress and trying to become a better person."

"And how is that?"

"All these keys, secrets, tips, and frameworks I was following created palpable actions. My actions displayed improvement, which is literally antithetical to the acts that show blatant signs of people with dependencies, and even addictions."

"And did they ever notice your dependency?"

"No . . . or at least, nobody has said anything to my face. It's why the only person who could really realize it was *myself*."

Isabel nodded without giving a response. I drummed up a rant.

"My pursuit of self-improvement left a deep void of fulfillment and purpose that has plagued me for the past couple of years. Many of the actions, habits, and mentalities I had were quite detrimental to many aspects of my life that I truly cared about. I failed because I was pursuing things that weren't true to myself. I wasn't using my own compass, I was borrowing someone else's because I couldn't read mine. But in a sense, I could read, or at least take time to decipher my own, but I chose not to. I opted for replication of others, instead of a reflection of myself."

Isabel raised her hand, which I took as a symbolic gesture to shut my mouth. *The soothsayer has heard enough*! She let out a meditative hum and gathered her thoughts, still remaining in complete tranquility. The wind outside started to grow louder. My lower back started to twitch. It wasn't pain that I felt, it was more like a knot I needed to shake to get it untangled. My side of the bench had no back support, so I kept flexing my abs and adjusting my posture to avoid the twitch. Isabel stopped humming.

"Sammy," she softly spoke. "Why did you listen to these people? These external sources?"

I furrowed my brow. "I already told you. They're thought leaders. People with the same problems as us, people who were in the same position as us once, people who dug themselves out of the pit we're all trapped in. We all need to get out, and they're the only ones with the ladder."

Her face went expressionless. "We're not talking about people trapped in the pit," she corrected with a seemingly gentle tone. "We're talking about *you*. You're the only one in the pit."

She looked back down at the diagram and smiled.

"And it's much deeper than you think."

We were getting somewhere, and the caricaturist soothsayer image I had of her was beginning to melt away.

Isabel went into the kitchen to rinse out her cup using an aged, ragged brown rag to swivel around the inside of the cup. I sat there patiently, palms resting on my thighs. I felt like a prisoner who was called into the warden's office, thumbs twiddling in anticipation while the warden— taking his sweet time— prepared himself a scotch with square ice cubes. An open window in the kitchen was rustling the drape covering it. Isabel closed it and came back in the main room with a spotless mug.

"Sammy," she spoke softly. "If I wanted to learn how to play golf, who should I talk to?"

Definitely not me, I thought to myself. The last time I played was years ago at a three-hole back in my hometown. A couple of balls went in the hole, others into sand traps and small ponds, and one straight through a mobile home window. Needless to say, the middle-aged woman living there was not happy.

"You should probably send a carrier pigeon to Tiger Woods' house," I replied.

Isabel chuckled with a response, "And millions of other budding golf professionals would say the same."

She stood up and walked down the hall to open a closet and came back with a tall angle broom and a small foam ball. She handed both of them to me. She grabbed her cup off the table and walked over to the other side of the main room and placed it sideways on the ground.

"Sammy," she said. "Show me how to play golf."

"I'm sorry?"

"Trust me, it's important."

I shrugged.

What in the hell is the purpose of this?

I clutched the broom and placed the foam ball on the ground, directly in line with the mouth of the cup.

"So, this is called putting," I demonstrated to Isabel.

"What's that?"

"It's a type of stroke in golf. It's when your ball is close enough to the hole that you want to gently tap it in."

"And why do I want to get the ball in the cup?"

"So you can finish the hole."

"What does that mean?"

I could tell that Isabel was acting naive, but I also knew it was part of the exercise. I explained all the rules of golf to her— how to keep score, what a stroke was, the different kinds of clubs, the different 'holes,' the silly-looking pastel-colored polos, and most importantly, how to win.

I opened my stance and gently rested the bristles of the broom next to the ball.

"So, you want to have your feet shoulder-width apart," I said. "Have a comfortable grip on your club, or broom, in this case, and gently rock your hands forward."

I demonstrated. The broom bristles tapped the foam ball toward the cup. I missed by a fork's length. I picked up the cup and sat back down at the table. Isabel smiled.

"Do you think you successfully taught me how to play golf?"

"I think I did the best I could."

She smiled again. "Now, can you teach me something else?"

"Like what?"

"Can you teach me about the true meaning of life and how I can live my life to the fullest?"

I stumbled. "Uhhh . . . I'm not sure how to answer that."

She stroked her chin. "Are you not an expert?"

"Not by any measure," I said with a faint laugh.

Isabel hummed. "If you're not an expert, then who should I talk to?"

"I don't know. Maybe a psychologist? A psychiatrist? A life coach?" I chuckled. "Probably someone with a bunch of inspirational quotes hung up on their wall."

Isabel beveled her cheeks. "Many others would agree with you, but I want to explain why that may be a flawed approach."

I was skeptical. "Well, then who can teach us how to live our lives? Who can we trust or listen to?"

Isabel remained peaceful yet insightful in her speech.

"We can't teach each other how to correctly live life, but we can teach each other how to correctly play golf."

The same thought rushed into my head. *What the hell is she talking about?* I thought about this notion. To me, it made no sense, but maybe Isabel was here to make it logical. I nodded and asked her to elaborate. She gave me a crisp smile.

"Golf experts can teach us how to correctly play the sport of golf, because golf is manufactured and governed by artificial laws we've created. People created the rules, the required equipment, and the measure to determine great play, or in other words, the scoreboard. We know a birdie is a good score, and a bogey is a less than desirable score. It's why you were able to teach me how to play golf."

"I see."

"We should listen to experts if we want to learn golf, photography, magic, welding, microeconomics, public speaking, sales, or coding. We have established objective parameters for learning these subjects and skills. In this case, listening to an expert is wise, if not *mandatory*, to become exceptional."

"But why can't we do the same with people who are experts on living life? Why can I listen to Phil Mickelson teaching me how to shoot out of a sand trap, and not a life coach about how to live my life to the fullest?"

"Life coaches, spiritual gurus, or whatever title you want to give them, cannot teach us how to correctly play the game of life. Life experts didn't create the rules, the required equipment, or the measure to determine great play because these were all created by nature. Even as a culture, we have such bifurcated knowledge on how we should live. There isn't one axiom that we can reference as the ultimate blueprint for how we should carry out our lives. We don't have a universal agreement on the meaning, and it's a subject we may never be able to explain, since the explanation itself would eliminate the need for the question in the first place. The rules of life are more subjective and the experts know as much about following them as you do. Yes, an expert may be able to guide you to properly function in the life that we as humans have constructed for ourselves, but our existence is more complex than that."

I prodded her. "But can't you argue on behalf of evolution? That the meaning of life is to survive long enough to pass on your genes?"

Isabel smiled. "You could, but you could also argue that we've outgrown that meaning as a species. Sex is now mostly for pleasure instead of passing genes, and survival has been muddled, as we are the only species that practice non-altruistic suicide. If we want to dig deeper psychologically, we're also the only species who will take the lives of others because we don't know how to live our own. But the deeper question to ask is whether we are still operating our lives by the laws of nature, or if we've outgrown them and created our own? Nonetheless, in both cases, we still don't have an agreement on what those rules are."

I still wasn't sold. Skepticism ran through my body. "What do you mean, we don't have an agreement on the rules of life? We have laws and ethics and codes of conduct."

Isabel hummed to herself. "Yes, we do. But none of them are absolute or universally agreed upon. We know how to cure smallpox, polio, and measles, but we don't know whether we should make abortion legal or illegal. We know how to send humans to the moon and space probes out into the depths of our solar system, but we don't know if we should allow euthanasia. There isn't an absolute argument or law on abortion, euthanasia, or any other issues that dictate the lives of humans that we can all agree on. We just can't come to a clear consensus on how we should live."

"Yeah . . . sure. But we do have some sense of what's a good life. We don't classify people in mental hospitals, people addicted to drugs, people in jail, or people born into poverty as living so-called good lives."

"Yes, but again, these measures of life are based on the constructs that we have created. We objectively associate prison and poverty as bad, because we've created these stigmas in our head. One could also argue the same with psychosis and addiction."

"Okay, then how does one live a fulfilled life?"

Isabel smiled and gently grasped my hand from across the table and looked into my eyes. "Do you know why we are the most powerful and the most cursed species to walk this planet?"

I had no idea. And the hamster running on the intellectual hamster wheel in my head must have fallen off by now. Isabel took my perplexed facial expression as a response. She let go of my hand.

"Take a female sockeye salmon, for example. Bursting into the world from an orange circular egg. She comes into this world mobile but defenseless, with a yolk sack attached to her body for food. Her first task is to *survive*. To avoid being eaten by birds and other fish. If she survives, she becomes larger and her yolk sack shrinks. Her new task is to go out and find food. And still *survive*. If she does, she becomes even larger up to the level to become a spawner. Her new task is to reproduce. And *survive*. She migrates back to a river and finds a mate. When she does, she digs a nest at the bottom of the river and deposits thousands of eggs from her body before her mate comes over and fertilizes the eggs. When spawning is complete, she dies shortly after, becoming food for other animals whose purpose is to consume them for nourishment to survive long enough to reproduce. Now, the next cycle of sockeye salmons can begin.

"You see, Sammy. Not once in the salmon's life does she think to herself *'Why am I doing this? What is the purpose of doing this? Maybe I should do something else.'* This is a privilege she does not have. Her purpose is ingrained so deeply that the questions will never arise. *But we have this privilege.*

"We can ask ourselves these questions. We can walk a different path and we can disobey our biological responsibilities to create our own purpose. This is why we are so powerful. We have the power to choose our own meaning of life. But this is also why we are cursed.

"I can tell you about the meaning of life not just for the sockeye salmon. I can tell you the meaning of life for the elephant, the dolphin, the coyote, the hermit crab, or the eagle. For any other species that roams this earth we all share, I can tell you the meaning of life. But *we*, with our unmatched power of conscience— to ask questions previously unasked— we cannot come to an agreement. And that's the curse.

"Isn't that a tragedy? We are the only species in the world that can ponder the meaning of life but with this power, we can answer that question for every species on the planet except our own."

She said it more like a statement than a question. We sat in uncomfortable silence for a moment. I was trying to wrap my head around everything. Like a philosophical turban.

Isabel exhaled and smiled, staring at me with her marble eyes. "You should instead ask yourself '*How do I live a fulfilled life?*' It's the best you can do. To understand your pains and how to live a fulfilled life, you must look inward and try to create one not because it's *good*, but because it's *meaningful*."

I could see her point. Life had become more complex than ever. Our programming was out of date, making the purpose of life more obscure. Since we have a muddled understanding of our purpose as a species, we now alter ourselves to chase vague goals and milestones. Instead of looking for a mate or looking to survive, we are now chasing more amorphous goals that we continuously describe as growth, success, or fulfillment that hold little to no substance. I didn't have goals that were intrinsic to myself, I had extrinsic goals that would look appealing to others. I tackled *good* pains and goals, yet ignored my own *meaningful* pains and goals.

"I want to live a meaningful life, Isabel," I said. "I really do."

Isabel smiled.

"We have some housekeeping to do."

Isabel picked up the empty cup from the table and cashed in my two-day-old offer to help her in the kitchen. I obliged. There was a stack of dirty plates and utensils sitting in a plastic green tub. I grabbed one of the dirty plates and rinsed it under the sink for a few seconds before Isabel stopped me. She grabbed the plate out of my hand and handed me a single cup of hot cocoa, a different one. One that was sitting on the dirty dish rack for a while now. Also, *what time was it?*

"Just clean this, Sammy. I'll take care of the rest."

She began scrubbing and I looked at the cup. The inside of the cup was stained with brown streaks.

"Why are we doing the dishes now? In the middle of the night?"

She smiled and said nothing, continuing to scrub away the leftover food from the plates and utensils. I filled the cup with water and scrubbed the inside with a dirty sponge in a circular motion. The stains wouldn't come out. I wouldn't give up, so I kept scrubbing.

Isabel kept tending the dirty dishes on the rack, occasionally borrowing the faucet to run water over the dishes when I wasn't using it.

"This is all so weird," I said. "This must be the longest and most vivid dream I've ever had."

Isabel was silent, scrubbing the crusty leftover remnants of ketchup from a white porcelain dish.

"I've tried keeping a dream journal, but that didn't work out."

"Why not?" Isabel asked, coming out of her silent dishwashing groove.

"Kept forgetting. I read this online article once, I think it was from some health website. But apparently, when we wake up, we forget our entire dream within 10 minutes."

"That's interesting," Isabel said in a less-than-interested tone.

"Yeah, it's nuts. Like, how do you expect me to keep a dream journal, when I'll forget the contents of my dream by the time I open the cap?"

"I wouldn't expect it."

"I know. But this dream, or whatever this is, it's much more vivid, much longer, more clear. I feel like when I wake up, I won't forget this in 10 minutes."

"Maybe you can write about it in your journal."

"Or I can write a book about it."

Isabel looked over at me. I was scrubbing the inside of the cup with no success. The brown streaks seemed to look back at me and merely snicker.

She stopped me. "Not like this, use the other side of the sponge."

I flipped the sponge over from the soft yellow side to the harder green side and started to scrub. The brown streaks began coming off. Isabel smiled and went back to cleaning the plates.

"Hmm . . . a book," Isabel said. "That could be interesting."

"Yeah, it could. It could help people. But then again, I wouldn't be much different from any of those people I just criticized."

I put the cup on the dry rack with Isabel's completed dishes. I wiped my hands dry with the raggedy blue hand towel.

"I can already see myself prancing around the Amazon search results, promising people how I'm unique and different from everyone else."

"But it could be different," Isabel said. She was scrubbing the black stains out of an old metal pot. The silver finish was worn and almost overtaken by the brown rust.

"What do you mean?" I asked. "How could it be different?"

Isabel put some extra elbow grease into the pot, until the inside seemed as clean as it could possibly get. She grabbed the raggedy blue hand towel from my side and started wiping down the inside.

"Do you understand that writing a novel like this comes with a form of responsibility to bestow knowledge?"

"Yeah, sure I'd agree with that. But I feel like I'd be no different."

I grabbed some paper towels off the roll, stood up by a wooden stick, and started wiping the water off my side of the kitchen counter. "Nowadays, anyone with an opinion and a subpar Wi-Fi connection can bestow their wisdom onto the world. Would I become that same person who leverages the printing press instead of the radio waves? What gives me the right to produce a hypothetical novel worthy of anyone's attention?"

The question was rhetorical, but Isabel decided to answer anyway. She smiled, putting the dry (and relatively clean) pot on the drying rack.

"I think you know the answer to that question better than I do. What would you want to share?"

I started with a stammer. "I— I mean like . . . I don't know off the top of my head. I think *I'd want to share a story.*"

I ended with booming confidence in my voice. "One that may resonate with the reader in some way. My story wouldn't have a guaranteed output or feeling that someone should have when they're done reading it."

The faucet was running, its knob turned all the way to the left, pointing to the label HOT in bright red text.

"That sounds pretty holistic," Isabel noted as she rinsed around the sink, pushing the remaining pieces of food and dirt down the drain. "What topic do you have in mind?"

"No clue," I told her. My area of the kitchen was completely dry. I balled up the rest of the damp paper towels and tossed them in a nearby trash can. "I just wouldn't want to pick some modern trailblazing topic that would get me the eyeballs needed to sign a book deal, so I could live off the royalties in Indonesia. *No thanks.* That life holds no meaningful value to me, and I would first have to drown in boredom and live devoid of fulfillment on the warm, sandy beaches of Bali to really understand that."

Isabel shut the faucet off. "But what about the story?"

"I'm not sure yet," I stammered. "Could be about anything."

Isabel smiled and started drying off the cleaned dishes with a raggedy blue hand towel.

"But you already know what it's *not* about."

"I know it's not about others. I know it's about myself."

"But it's not only that."

"What?"

"It's not about a framework or a set of principles. It's not about secrets, tricks, hacks, rules, rituals, or anything of that sort."

"Right, I'm not sharing any foolproof formula or principle for anyone to use."

"Yes. You understand blindly applying principles and actions. Just because they worked for someone else, it wouldn't mean they *wouldn't* have a self-destructive outcome."

"Like Medusa installing a mirror in her bathroom, because someone told her it would boost her self-confidence."

Isabel chuckled. Before tonight, I would never have guessed that Isabel would understand a joke about Greek mythology.

"Sammy," she said. "Your aptitude is irrelevant. Your perceived lack of experience is irrelevant. You're not sharing a framework for life, *you're sharing a story*."

Then, another silence swept over us. Isabel took the cup from the drying rack. I had scrubbed the inside of it with so much brute force, that I polished off some of the color. She chuckled as if she heard another clever Medusa joke.

"Don't worry, Sammy. I have plenty more cups like that."

Once Isabel was pleased with how everything looked in the kitchen, the dishes and utensils sitting correctly in the drying rack, the raggedy towels neatly folded, the kitchen counter thoroughly wiped down and dry, we went back into the main room and sat at the wooden table.

The box still sat in the middle and Isabel picked it up with both hands, glancing at the third lock.

She placed the box back in the center of the table and hummed. "We're almost there, Sammy."

I stared at the last lock, wondering how I could lift the latch. We sat in silence for what it seemed like an eternity. It felt like 30 minutes, but it very well could have just been five. Time moves slower when you're doing nothing and just observing. Isabel had her eyes closed, meditatively humming to herself. I sat with my elbow on the table and my chin resting in the palm of my hand.

Was she waiting for me to say something?

I was becoming hyper-vigilant about everything around me. Everything could have some sort of meaning. This dream, or whatever it was, could be giving me hints of clues. Or it wasn't. And Isabel was just waiting for me to speak.

Say something.

I cleared my throat and Isabel slowly opened one eye, flexing her eyebrow.

"The pit—" I started to tell her. "The one we're all trapped in. The one *I'm* trapped in."

Both of her eyes were open now. "Yes?"

"You said it was deeper."

She shook her head. "No, I didn't say that." She had fixed herself another cup of hot cocoa, using the cup with the color slightly polished off, thanks to my scrubbing skills. She took a small sip and put the cup down. Faint trails of steam were rising from the top. She sat back against the wall and smiled.

"Sammy," she said. "I said that the pit was *much deeper.*"

———

Isabel jolted my gaze with a punching statement. *How deep in the pit do you think you are?* I had no clue. I thought I was deep enough as it was. I couldn't seem to muster an answer. She shook her head at me.

"You're struggling to share your story, because you haven't changed your mind."

My body jolted again. "What?"

Isabel smiled. "Charles Atterley once said that the world will be saved by people with changed minds, not programs. The world won't be saved by people with old minds and new programs. Does that make sense?"

"That makes zero sense to me."

Isabel flashed another crisp smile and kept her buoyant aura, ready to give me another insightful lecture.

"We need to differentiate between minds— specifically vision and programs."

"Visions and programs?"

"Yes, many times we think they're the same, but in reality, they are completely different."

I scratched the back of my neck and muttered a complied "Okay." She flashed a smile.

"Programs are rules and guidelines we follow to carry out a certain behavior. For example, emission trading and carbon emission cap programs create behavior to reduce pollution. Fitness programs create behavior to lose weight. Wildlife safety programs create behavior to preserve animals."

"Okay.

"But programs won't save us. Emission trading and carbon emission cap programs won't save the world from global warming. Fitness and healthy eating programs won't save people from obesity. Wildlife safety and protection programs won't save animals from extinction."

My skepticism bubbled to the surface. I challenged her.

"I don't agree with that. Programs can be really helpful. Like, what you said about emission trading programs. Those can help control pollution. Also, the wildlife safety programs can reduce poaching and people destroying habitats. There are programs that help."

Isabel nodded. "Yes, that is true. But the fundamental point I am making here, one that Atterley pointed out, is that to enact radical change, *you need a new vision, not a new program.*"

"Ok, but that still doesn't address my point about programs."

Isabel raised a kind eyebrow at me. I started to act more defensive than inquisitive. I couldn't tell if this was good or bad in her eyes. Inevitably, she returned to her calm and centered self, showing off a crisp smile.

"New visions," Isabel explained, "are self-sustaining while programs are designed to counter that vision. Pollution and the destruction of resources to create fuel and power is a vision of our culture. As we live, we will continue to carry out these acts without the use of any programs. But if we want people to use renewable resources, recycle, and cut back on waste, we need to enact programs or pass legislation to stimulate that behavior."

"I see."

"Programs are vital, but the encouragement of certain behavior that's against the visions in our culture is stimulated by programs. PETA and the Wildlife Prevention Act are programs that help preserve wildlife, but if our culture changed its mind and adopted the vision that animals are equal in nature, do you think we would have built cities, neighborhoods, strip malls, and factories on top of their habitats and placed them in zoos just for sheer entertainment?"

"I— I guess not," I stammered for a bit. "But what does all of this have to do with my story? Or even me getting out of this pit?"

"You've realized this already from your experience consulting external sources. You can't address your pains and help yourself with a program. No framework, principle, or guideline will change that. But your vision— a self-sustaining one that believes that you can address and remedy your pains— can change that."

"My vision? I don't understand and I don't see how this relates to the last lock or any of the other locks on this box."

Isabel smiled.

"Sammy, I didn't randomly choose the order of these locks. They flow downstream into one another like an estuary. The first lock is about understanding that you, as a person, can experience pain and suffering, despite who you are or how you were raised. The second lock is about accepting that these pains you are experiencing can be malignant, despite seeming objectively benign to everything around you. The third lock is about changing your vision— one that gives yourself the power to understand these pains and to not let a lack of aptitude, skill, or experience derail your true understanding of them."

I couldn't utter any words, so I fell silent as she rolled the last few words off her tongue. I couldn't fix, I mean *understand* (I could hear Isabel correcting me in my head) my pains because of my vision. I held a vision that I didn't have the power to understand my pains, and that I needed someone else to help me or do the work for me.

"Now Sammy," Isabel softly spoke, "how do we completely open this box?"

I thought for a second until I mustered up the intellectual courage to synthesize her point in my own words.

"Can I address each lock?"

Isabel gave me a proud nod with her head. To her, it seemed like I was becoming better at truly understanding myself, but she clearly wanted me to figure out everything on my own. I took a deep breath.

"I— I need to accept that these pains are valid, despite who I am or how I was raised. I need to accept that I am now able to see them."

"Yes, Sammy, that's the first lock. Now, the second one."

"I need to accept that these pains can be detrimental to myself, even if they aren't objectively categorized that way."

"Yes, that's good. And the last lock?"

"I need to accept that I have the power to address and understand these pains, *despite* who I am or what I've experienced."

With a short gaze and a joyful smile, Isabel placed the box in her hand, and lifted the latch up on the third lock.

She kept her hands firmly around the box, keeping it closed. I could hear the wind outside rustling the branches of the trees, followed by the same sound of a distant gong until it faded. I had an urge to ask Isabel a question I should have asked a while ago. So, I bluntly asked her.

"What are you?"

She was staring down at the box. She tilted her head up to me. I peered into her dark marble eyes.

"What do you mean, Sammy?"

"Like, are you a ghost? A representation of something? Is this just one big dream?" I scanned the room around, opening my arms and displaying the main room to her, as if I was a realtor. She formed her lips in a U-shape, bulging out her cheeks.

"I'm Isabel," she said with conviction. "*Your* Isabel, to be precise."

"Yeah, okay sure. You look and sound like her, but you really aren't her. You're a different kind of Isabel, or you're not Isabel at all."

She kept her smile. "You shouldn't focus so much on this—"

I interrupted. "Yeah, I know, but like, I kinda don't care as much. I'm just curious now."

Her smile slowly faded. Her lips straightened. "Do you really want to know who I am?" she said in a punctured but ominous tone. "You wouldn't listen to me if you did."

I stammered "I'm— I'm not sure. Should I?"

We sat in another prolonged silence until a *slurping* sound from Isabel filled the room. She put her cup of cocoa down and smiled at me with her dark marble eyes.

"Do you have a better question?" she asked, matching my level of certainty. And I did, I indeed had a better question for her.

"Okay," I started. "Why are you helping me?"

Isabel smiled and let out a small chuckle. "I'm not, Sammy." She picked up her cup, dropped it in the sink, and returned to the table.

"You're helping yourself. I'm merely guiding you in the right direction." She looked into my eyes. "You're a stubborn horse, but only you can drink the water from the trough." Isabel then looked back down at the box, with all the latches finally opened up.

"And it seems you've already taken a few sips."

Chapter 5

All three latches were unlocked, but Isabel hesitated to open the box. "We've been sitting for a long time," she said. "Let's go for a walk."

I looked back outside through the large window. It was dark, but not pitch black. The *pueblo* seemed to be illuminated by streetlamps and house lights.

She handed me the box and instructed me specifically not to open it. I palmed it with one of my hands as we left the house through the blue behemoth and into the small *pueblo*.

The air felt different compared to when we walked around earlier in the night– it was denser this time. The wind rustled the trees, causing an abundance of leaves to sway back and forth in the air. There was a deep silence in the town, as if it was recently evacuated.

I couldn't hear anything, not even a hum of static buzzing from the streetlights. The patrol cars and kids playing jacks in the streets had all completely vanished. I didn't see a single passing car kicking up smoke from the dirt roads.

We walked for what felt like 20 minutes until we reached the main plaza of Villa Diaz Ordaz. There was a small park, post office, police station, and a beautiful cathedral church. All of them were closed and vacated.

The dead silence remained. We found a white bench for both of us in the main plaza that overlooked a large patch of farmland with a silhouette of the mountain range in the background.

We sat for a moment in silence while Isabel hummed. I'm quite fidgety and anxious when there isn't anything to distract me, so I started pinching together dirt, rubbing the bits in between my index and thumb. It was a better alternative to pulling the hair out of my scalp, after all. Isabel noticed what I was doing and chuckled.

"You can never stay still, can you?" she said with a smile.

"Never. You know this better than I do."

"And you know this about yourself."

I smiled and let the bits of dirt fall from my fingers to the ground. I rubbed the palms of my hands together to keep them warm— the wind made it chillier outside than I expected. Isabel beveled her cheeks at me.

"Sammy," she said in a soft-spoken tone. "Now that we've removed the locks, I'd like to tell you a story."

I obliged with a friendly nod. I didn't feel like vocalizing anything after sitting in a long period of silence.

"On a cold autumn morning in New York, the people of Manhattan were going about their day when Central Park was visited by an unlikely guest. A Mandarin duck had suddenly appeared in the Central Park pond, swimming in harmony with the other mallards in the water. Normally, no one would think twice to stop and look at a new duck, but the Mandarin duck was special. It donned an array of beautiful colors— a bright red bill with a purple breast and orange wings. On the sides, it was streaked with white and black, and its feathers extended past its neck, radiating a darkish green. It looked as if it was brought to life from a children's coloring book. Within hours, the duck became a celebrity among the people of Manhattan. The

Mandarin was native to i East Asia, so it was odd to see one in a New York City pond. There was a lot of speculation as to how the duck arrived. It may have escaped from a local aviary, or it could have been released in the pond by its owner. Regardless of how it came, people were captivated by its looks. On that day, hundreds flooded to the pond to see such a beautiful creature bask in its natural habitat."

I waited for Isabel to continue, since I assumed the story wasn't over, but she fell silent with a crisp smile on her face.

"Is that the whole story?" I asked.

She didn't answer. She kept her hands placed on her lap and continued to stay in meditative thought.

"Is that really it?" I prodded. She stayed silent.

"I don't get why you would tell me that story. It wasn't even a real story. It sounded like you just read it from a newspaper."

Isabel remained silent with a gleeful smile still spread across her face. I was still confused, unsure if the story was supposed to have a hidden meaning. I kept thinking that this was some sort of canary in a coal mine.

"How was that a story?" I asked rhetorically. "Stories have characters, plots, twists, climaxes, a journey, an adventure, a challenge, a reward. You just talked about how a bunch of people swarmed Central Park to see a pretty duck."

"Do you not find it odd?" she asked, finally speaking up.

"Find what odd? That a bunch of people dropped everything they were doing to go look at a pretty duck?"

"Not only that, but *why* they dropped everything to see it."

"I don't know, because it looked pretty? I mean, I'd go check it out as well, I guess, if I lived in New York."

Isabel nodded. "Yes, there was no other reason to go see the duck, aside from the fact that it looked pretty."

"By the way you described it, I would agree."

"But the Mandarin duck wasn't any different from the Mallards that accompanied the pond with it."

"What do you mean?"

"It didn't have any unique skills that made it different. It couldn't perform backflips or run a synchronized aquatic dance. At the end of the day, it's just a duck."

"Yeah, but it's a different species of duck, one that people don't get to see too often in their daily lives."

"So why did people swarm to go see it?"

"Because it was beautiful."

"But it's not just *physical* beauty, Sammy. It's deeper than that. It always is."

I hesitated for a second before letting the next thought in my head ooze out of my mouth. I decided to think about my words carefully. This seemed like a good tactic going forward.

"I don't understand," I told her. "I don't see how this is different from beautiful places like the Eiffel Tower or Stonehenge or anywhere else. Every year, thousands of people drop everything to visit these places. We're attracted to physical beauty."

"Yes, Sammy, that may be true," Isabel replied. "But places like the Eiffel Tower and Stonehenge have much more than physical beauty— they have beauty in their history, influence, and culture.

Someone visits Stonehenge instead of the Eiffel Tower not only because of its physical beauty, but also because of its *hidden* beauty. The important aspect to understand here with the Mandarin duck is *absence*."

When that last word rolled off her tongue, all I could think about was the *pueblo*. I looked around. The absence of people, the sounds they make, and the life they bring to the community. The village was barren without people.

"Okay, then, how does the duck relate to *absence*?" I asked. "If anything, the Mallard is more related to *absence* since it didn't have anything that made it interesting enough for people to flock to it."

Isabel smiled. She seemed pleased that I wasn't accepting her words as biblical text, and that I was using a bit of scrutiny. "The purpose of my story wasn't to talk about a time when hundreds of people dropped everything to take pictures of a colorful duck," she affirmed.

"Then what was the point?"

"To demonstrate an archetype of misperception."

I gave her a blank stare. My brain couldn't connect the dots. Isabel must have understood the puzzlement on my face since she tried to explain her concept further.

"I think it would be easier if I compared the two. Imagine two types of labels— *Mandarins and Mallards*."

I nodded like a student in primary school.

"*Mandarins* are emblematic of everything we see as better. It's the physical metaphor of the proverb, 'the grass is always greener on the other side.' We perceive them as proper, put together, and *absent* of any lifestyle blemishes or boils. It always appears that they're looking at life through rose-tinted glasses and don't carry any heavy burdens on their backs. You see people who have the visual elements of a perfect life and you think to yourself that they've shed the skin of all their problems. *Mallards,* on the other hand, are the antithesis to Mandarins. In the animal kingdom, they're the most common species of duck and they don't carry any of the flashy physical features that the Mandarins possess. They're seen as ordinary, with nothing extraordinary, noteworthy, or unique about them. Sometimes, we even see them as broken or beneath us."

"I see."

"But here's the misperception— *Mandarins and Mallards are both ducks.* And aside from physical representation, they're really no different from each other. As I said, the Mandarin can't perform backflips or run a synchronized aquatic dance, nor can the Mallard."

"Okay, I see what you're painting here, but what does this have to do with me?"

"You said that you removed certain faults that were validated not by you, but by others?"

"Yes, I did," I replied while thinking of all the times I wielded the blade *Occam's Chisel* near my face after comparing myself to others, percolating my imperfections to the surface.

"And how will you know that the pains you wish to address are true to yourself and not influenced by others?"

I scratched the back of my neck. I flexed my eyebrows and hummed to myself, trying to put myself in some form of deep philosophical thought. Then, my hand went straight for my hair, until I smacked it away with the other.

"I'm not sure," I told her. "But I do know there are aspects about myself that are keeping me from who I want to be."

"And when will you know that you have become who you want to be?"

"When I see my reflection in the water and don't spit at it," I jokingly replied. Isabel didn't look amused by this answer.

"My Sammy," she said. "I'm here to guide you toward understanding your true pain and suffering. My allegory about the Mandarin duck isn't arbitrary, it's actually quite fundamental. It may even be the most important aspect of your journey since it's the foundational layer that everything else is built on top of."

"I can see that, Isabel. But I still don't get your point."

"You approached these external sources because there were aspects of your life you wanted to address. However, after comparing yourself to someone else, more aspects of your life suddenly became drawbacks. Your perception of the world around you was full of Mandarins and you saw yourself as a Mallard. Before we can understand your pain and suffering, we need to make sure it's based on an internal observation of yourself instead of an external comparison of others."

I could finally understand her point. I put people on pedestals who had physical attributes of happiness and success, and that was, indeed, quite detrimental to me. But at the same time, I couldn't blame the people who chose those physical attributes. We're so heavily influenced by how people will perceive us, that sometimes, we want to *look* happy and successful rather than actually being a function of these properties. Rolex can probably take the batteries out of all their watches, and people will still flock to the stores and buy them.

"We want to focus on the true pains," Isabel affirmed. "Not the ones that percolated to the surface when you consulted external sources."

"Yeah, that's what I've been trying to do for some time."

Isabel smiled. "Now we must address *uncertainty*."

UNCERTAINTY

The church bells rang at the top of the hour. A small flock of birds evicted from a nearby tree, startled by the noise. I looked over at the mountain silhouette. I was mesmerized, but Isabel didn't look quite as enthralled. She must have been used to seeing landscapes like this. Looking at the vast mountain range percolated a question in my head.

"When will I know I have become who I want to be?"

Isabel gave a pleasant look, but ignored my question. It was her turn to look at the mountain silhouette. I felt uncomfortable with the question floating in the air unanswered. She hummed and volleyed the question back to me.

"When I am happy, fulfilled, and at peace with myself," I replied.

She didn't seem to be too keen about my vagueness, but it was clearly a better answer than my previous one.

"Are you certain about that?" she asked.

I exhaled. "If I had to be honest, no, I'm not."

She smiled. *"Uncertainty is psychologically unpleasant."*

I gave her a perplexed look. I asked her why she kept saying that phrase with such emphasis. She turned her attention away from the mountain silhouette and back towards me.

"Sammy," she said. "You won't grow as a person unless you embrace the unknowns of the future. Do you understand this?"

I did. I understood that jumping headfirst into uncertainty came with addressing the harsh realities of the world— that life could feel like a maladaptive video game with unlimited levels and no true end.

"To an extent, I would say that I do."

Isabel grinned. "And to what extent is that?"

"I understand that nothing in the world is certain and that nothing is definite. Things will inevitably go wrong in all aspects of my life."

"I see."

"I understand that women will break my heart, companies will reject my resume, and reality will rob me of my high fidelity of flawlessness."

Isabel smiled at me. "You understand that this whole process of self-reflection could topple over and collapse on itself, or it could set the foundation for myself to become a better person in my own eyes. Both outcomes are probable—"

I interrupted. "But I had to embrace the fact that I wouldn't know which one would triumph over the other."

Isabel smiled a rare smile, one with her teeth flashing. "We have to set realistic expectations... and it seems that you have already done so."

DISSOCIATION

Isabel spent a few moments looking at the mountain silhouette. In the period of silence, I blunted the urge to pull my hair by picking up small heaps of dirt off the ground instead. I pinched the rocks and other minerals, rubbed them together, and let them fall to the ground. Then, another question struck me.

"How can I find my true pains?" I asked.

Isabel interrupted her gaze and focused back on me.

"What do you mean, Sammy?"

"Well, we want to unearth the pains that came from an internal understanding instead of an external comparison, right?"

"Yes, that's right. But we should also specify that we aren't addressing pains related to physical ailments or bodily dysfunctions. The advancement of technology and medicine can intervene and remedy the majority of these pains for us, without the need for intrinsic reflection."

I occasionally flexed my eyebrows when Isabel started to sound like a research paper, but I never prodded her on it. There were already enough unanswered questions for me to tackle.

"Yeah, that makes sense," I told her as I continued to pick up small bits of dirt from the ground, pinching the rocks and minerals with my thumb and index finger, and letting them fall to the ground.

"But how do we separate them out? How do we *dissociate* them from each other?"

Isabel watched me play with the dirt and smiled. "Sammy," she said. "There are many aspects about yourself that you want to address, so in a way, you already have a sense of what those pains are. So, I ask you, how would you unearth your true intrinsic pains?"

I noticed what looked like dirty blue topaz gemstone partially covered in the dirt. It was no larger than an American dime and looked as if it had been stitched to an article of clothing.

"I don't know," I replied as I picked up the gemstone and pinched it between my fingers. "The pains I believed I had when consulting external sources felt all too real for me to just dissociate from."

Isabel took a deep breath, followed by a long exhale. Then, she flexed her lips toward her ears.

"You need to create attributes," she said.

I looked up at her. Isabel noticed the gemstone in my hands. She clasped her hands together and smiled. "You were able to pick this gemstone out from the dirt because it has attributes— characteristics that you could identify apart from the millions of other minerals sifting in the sand."

I sat there with a blank expression. My right leg started to tremble, and my lip started to quiver. I looked deeply into the gemstone, watching the bright blue kaleidoscope patterns dance with each other in symphonic harmony. Isabel put her hand on my knee.

"I understand it's hard. You said you want to be happy, fulfilled, and at peace with yourself. What is keeping you from attaining those aspects of your life?"

I sighed. "I still don't know..."

"Let's take a step back. How did you identify the true pain in your life that you wanted to rectify most?"

I continued to examine the gemstone. "Well, I looked at the pains that I fundamentally held before external sources were used to help me. They're the ones that kept reappearing and have stayed constant for a long period of my life."

Isabel nodded. "I believe the important criteria here is *recurrence*. What do you think?"

I told her it was fair. She asked what else I looked at.

"I mean," I said. "I would say pains that created, well— the ones that created *pain*, they're the ones that inflicted mental and sometimes physical atrophy."

Isabel nodded again. "The second important criteria here seems to be *damage*."

"Yes, *recurrence* and *damage*. I would say that those are the two most crucial attributes."

"And will you know for certain that using these two criteria will work to filter out your true intrinsic pains?"

"No, but I believe I've looked at my pains in the most holistic possible way. These aren't set in stone, but it's a start."

Isabel smiled. "*Uncertainty is psychologically unpleasant. And embracing uncertainty is the only way to make it less unpleasant.*"

I smiled back and stuffed the gemstone in my pocket as a small token of this *pueblo* that I possibly would never visit again. This eerily barren, deserted, quiet, and beautiful *pueblo*.

Isabel looked to the silhouette of the mountain range before smiling and saying, "We're almost there. Soon, we can open the box."

CONVICTION

My attention shifted. I was no longer in a trance looking at the mountain silhouette. I had been staring at the box, making sure it was safe. My hands started to tremble at the thought of finally opening the lid.

Isabel interrupted my trance.

"We identified *recurrence* and *damage* as two helpful filters in identifying your true pains," she continued. "Now, we can start to understand what your true intrinsic pains are."

She looked at me with a gleeful smile as I thought to myself for a moment. Isabel had helped lead me all the way up to this point, so I assumed she would just keep going– that she would just lead me to the answers I needed.

I guess she wanted me to take the wheel. I clutched the box harder. She noticed my continued train of thought and added to her original question.

"I can't tell you what your true pains are, Sammy. I can only help lead you, so that *you* will eventually understand them."

She was right. I decided to stop tap dancing around the question and actually answer it. "Maybe I would want to understand who I am as a person, who I—"

Isabel interrupted me with a grunt. She flexed an eyebrow at me, but then decompressed herself.

"I said earlier that conviction is important."

"Yes, but you said it wasn't important at the moment."

"But here, it is most important. From here on out, your thoughts and ideas should be expressed with a high degree of conviction. Defer using *words of uncertainty* like 'maybe,' 'perhaps,' or 'I guess' at the beginning of your ideas. Do you know why this is important?"

This was especially vibrant in my life. I can't count the number of times I've made some profound claim or opinion, and then completely dismantled it by getting to the end and passively saying, 'I don't know.'

"I guess– sorry, I mean— I would say it's important, because if I don't, it feels like I don't even believe what I'm saying."

"Yes. Instead of owning the idea, it feels more like you're renting it and can give it up at any time. But there's another layer here to dig into— to understand what beliefs create. What do beliefs create, Sammy?"

"I'm not sure. But if I had to answer, I would say they help create your perception of reality."

"Yes, Sammy, that's quite true. But I'm not looking at what beliefs *help* create, but rather what they single-handedly *create*."

"I don't know."

"If I had a belief that you didn't like, what would most likely happen?"

"We would argue, or I would talk about why I disagree."

"Right. Beliefs create disagreements. But why is it important to have disagreements?" she asked.

"Again, I don't know."

Isabel gave a comforting look and remained patient with me.

"Sammy, what do disagreements create?"

"Changed beliefs, I guess?"

"Sometimes they do, and sometimes they don't. But what happens between disagreements and changed beliefs?

"A discussion?"

"Yes! They create *discourse*."

"And how is that important?

"Disagreements create discourse, and discourse breaks down the walls of your echo chamber. Discourse fights against the insulation of ideas. Discourse helps improve and enhance your views to better guide your life, even if your views are about yourself. Do you understand why this is important to what we're trying to do here today?"

"I'm not totally there yet."

"These pains we're about to examine, the way we frame and eventually understand and remedy them, are not written in stone. Your thoughts need to remain malleable. I put so much emphasis on *conviction,* because a lack of conviction with your beliefs reduces the likelihood of disagreements, which reduces the likelihood of discourse. This, in turn, keeps your beliefs insulated and unchanged."

"I see. But if I don't completely believe my own beliefs, who would want to even bother challenging them?"

"And if someone did?" Isabel inquired.

"Then I could just say that I didn't totally believe them in the first place, as long as I express them with a lack of conviction.

"Exactly. You want to be challenged on your beliefs, and using *words of uncertainty* deter people from that challenge."

"Ah, I see your point now."

"I think now is the time for us to truly start to understand your pains. The ones that are truly intrinsic in nature."

I looked up at the dark sky, which was speckled with stars. It was as if someone had sprinkled bits of salt over a blanket of freshly-paved asphalt. They glistened to the same cadence of my internal dialogue.

My pains seemed more prevalent than ever. The crescendoing music wasn't louder, but rather more sharp and clear. I could intuitively listen to the melody, for nothing was mumbled or distorted. It was as if I had an actual pianist living in my ear canal.

Isabel smiled. She gazed at the box and gestured for me to open it.

THE PAINS

I lifted up the lid of the box. Inside were three different objects.

The first was a circular, pocket-sized pop-up hairbrush with a mirror inside, coated with baby blue paint. The color popped out in the brown box, but the locket was beaten up, dirty, and the mirror inside was shattered.

The second object was a single chain link. It was similar in size and appearance to a carabiner, and its silver finish glistened in the moonlight. There was no visible damage to it.

The third artifact was a Ticonderoga pencil, but it was completely missing the lead point.

I took the artifacts out of the box to uncover a severed head of a green rose laying underneath everything. I had no idea what it symbolized, and it seemed like Isabel didn't have the inkling to tell me.

She simply smiled and looked up at the star-speckled sky in awe.

Chapter 6

December 9, 2018

I was 19 years old and halfway through my first year of college. The past four months were filled with gluttonous partying and irresponsibility. I had no concern over finding a job, internship, or career. My future didn't cross my mind once, and my roommates hated me for it.

I lived with six others split into two different rooms, with one shared bathroom. Three people lived in each room. They were all hardworking. Four of them were engineers, and one was on the pre-med track.

I, on the other hand, was a cultural arts major. I chose that major based on the light course load rather than my genuine interest. While their exams had questions about kinematics and probability, my exams asked us to write personal essays and make art pieces. They were overworked and under-slept, and in stark contrast, I was underworked and over-partying. We would often clash about the noise, the friends I would bring over, and the late hours in which I would be awake.

It wasn't until one night— specifically, Valentine's Day— that I had a cataclysmic realization. All my roommates were either out or with their partners, so it was the first time I was completely alone in the apartment.

*After 10 minutes, I broke down crying. I didn't cry because I was alone on Valentine's Day (which I saw as another Hallmark holiday), but rather because there was **nothing**.*

No noise, no people, no events, parties, plans, or opportunities. I realized that there was nothing to look forward to tomorrow. When everything was stripped away from me for a night, I was a purposeless individual, squandering my opportunities here in college.

There was nothing memorable about myself that I could explain to someone else.

In high school, I picked the skin off my lips from stress, but that urge thankfully went away immediately after I left for college.

This was the first time since then that I had felt the same level of stress and anxiety. But this time, my hands didn't go for my lips, they went for my scalp— twirling my hair, knotting the strands together, and pulling them out. After five minutes of unconscious hair-pulling, I pulled out a huge chunk of hair and held it in my hand.

I finally got my own attention, even if it wasn't through the best method.

I leapt out of bed and dug into my desk drawers to find something– anything– I could fiddle with. Coins, gum wrappers, untouched notebooks, notepads– they all went flying everywhere in my apartment.

I emptied everything out of the bottom drawer to uncover a bright blue circular object that was buried under everything. I opened the lid to see a circular mirror inside and a hairbrush that popped out on the other side. For a moment, I looked at my reflection in the intact mirror before popping the hairbrush out and brushing the knots out of my hair.

From that day on, I decided to take my career pursuit seriously.

———————

We sat on the white bench, continuing to admire the silhouette of the mountain. I placed the box (with the lid open) to my side and juggled the three objects in my hand.

The baby blue pop-up brush with the broken mirror, the silver chain link, and the pencil missing its point. I scratched my head looking at some of these objects. Isabel must have noticed.

"You look confused," she said.

"Very much," I told her.

Isabel looked pleased. "Do you recognize any of them?"

"Just one."

She smiled lightly and asked which one. I put the other objects back in the box and presented the pop-up brush in my hand. She inspected it for a moment and looked back at the mountain range. I lifted an eyebrow.

"So, what does it mean?" I prodded.

She turned her head toward me. "I'm not sure."

I furrowed my brow. "Shouldn't you know? You're the one guiding me through my pains."

"Yes, but I don't know your pains. Only *you* do. But I can tell you what these artifacts represent."

"You mean *objects*?"

She chuckled. "No, I mean *artifacts*."

She picked the pop-up brush out of my hand and fumbled with it between her fingers. "Each artifact represents a different pain in your life that you want to address."

She started wiping around the dirt on the surface of the pop-up brush with her thumb. "Each of them is in a condition that needs to be changed. Only after truly addressing the pain related to the artifact will they go back to their original conditions."

She handed the pop-up brush back to me and I held it in my hands. I felt its lightness in my palms– it was a round, plastic container no bigger than a wallet. I opened the lid and looked at my fragmented reflection in the shattered mirror.

"I don't know," I mumbled. "But I have a hunch."

Isabel smiled and gazed up at the night sky. I was still looking at myself in the broken mirror. I closed the lid down and held the pop-up brush in my hand. I sat up for a moment to stretch my back and distract myself from pulling out more of my hair.

I looked around the *pueblo*. The cathedral church caught my attention– it was magnificent. It must have been the tallest structure in the entire *pueblo*. During the day, it bustled with devout Oaxacan Christians— Isabel being one of them.

But tonight, it was empty. And besides the ring of the hourly bell, no sounds came from it.

I was interrupted from my staring when Isabel called my name, beckoning for me to return to the bench with her.

———

"Do you see the pain in your reflection?" she asked.

I fiddled with the pop-up brush in my hands. I gripped it between my index finger and thumb, looking at it as if it were an old penny. I opened the lid again to see the shattered mirror— all I saw staring back was my bifurcated reflection.

"It's not that I see the pain," I replied. "It's that I see the promise I made to myself so many years ago that led to the pain."

I slouched over myself, closed its lid, and pressed it against my temple. I let out a loud sigh and looked back up at Isabel. She smiled as she always did. Isabel offered to listen in a calm, soothing tone. I repositioned my back and kept the pop-up brush in my hands.

"A lot of pain in my life has come from the identification of myself," I replied. "I want to improve who I am as a person. I have battled with my identity for so many years, adopting some personalities that were inauthentic– and even downright damaging."

I sighed and relaxed my shoulders, pressing them against the back of the bench. Isabel smiled and looked up at the star-speckled sky.

"I think that's a good place to start," she said.

———

— JOURNAL ENTRY 2 —

November 11, 2018

I had no clue what to do with my career. After eight short months, I quit my first job out of college. I initially started in data entry until I was promoted to cold calling.

I wasn't cut out for sales, considering how much I hated trying to sell anything over the phone. So, I resigned without a formal backup. To make money, I took a job as a dog walker and as a part-time employee at Brookstone. Brookstone is (or was, since they may be bankrupt by now) a brick and mortar store that sells gadgets, gizmos, and lifestyle products that eventually become last-minute Christmas presents, and luckily for me, I joined in early December.

Despite the glaring fact that I was a college graduate from a highly prestigious university, working part-time at a retail store making $12 an hour, I put a humorous spin on the job to make it a bit more bearable.

The first task given to me by my penguin-shaped boss, Glen, was to memorize every single item we sold in the store so that I would know the exact function of every single gadget when customers asked. He threw a 200-page binder in my hands and instructed me to go to every corner of the store and memorize the characteristics of every product. I immediately ignored this ridiculous task and thought it would be much funnier if I made up facts about the products when customers asked. So, I did just that.

75-year-old man trying to buy the newest gizmo for his grandson for Christmas: How high up in the air can this drone fly up?

Me: I would say 30,000 feet. It also has a built-in mechanism that can make chocolate milk from scratch and deliver it to you.

Woman who is constantly cold: How hot does this heated blanket get?

Me: 500 degrees Kelvin, but only if you leave it on overnight.

Smart customer: Can I get a 10% discount?

Me: I like your confidence. I'll give you 30%.

Oh, I also gave discounts to attractive women and customers I had a good rapport with. Occasionally, foot traffic would decline, and the days would get slow. To make the time go quicker, I would also put on different characters and accents for every new encounter.

I once pretended to be a steward who took care of all the people who took advantage of sitting in the massage chairs without buying them. I would go up and ask them if they would like a fresh beverage, perhaps a Ginger Ale, and let them know that they would need to turn off their electronics, since the plane would be landing in about 20 minutes. Other times, I would go up to guests and ask them what year it was. When they responded, I would reply, "No way!" with a perplexed look on my face and walk away. This made a lot of people uncomfortable.

Glen disliked but tolerated my behavior. I frequently annoyed the living hell out of him, but I was still engaging with the customers, which he wanted. Also, people were lined up outside in droves trying to get a job at Brookstone, so he had to deal with me.

He eventually shifted his attitude, however. One day, as I was debuting my newest character on the sales floor (an undercover agent who worked at SkyMall), he waddled over to me (since his body resembled the spitting image of an Emperor penguin) until we were standing shoulder to shoulder. After watching me give (outstanding) pitches to customers about all the better deals at SkyMall and prompting them to leave the store, he leaned into my ear with his recently eaten ham sandwich breath and asked, "Do you think that's professional?"

Five months later, I quit and left a 200-page Brookstone product book on his desk wrapped up in a bright red bow.

In that moment and span of time, working for only $12 an hour, spending days stacking boxes of massage equipment in the storage room, running to the cafe across the street during my 10-minute break to shove a maple scone down my throat, mopping down the floors, and reorganizing all the products after hours, I felt more alive and more myself than almost any other time I could recall.

It felt like an authentic piece of my identity.

PASSION

Isabel asked me about my identity and the first recurrent and damaging aspect of my life that it was involved in. She asked in such a calm and passive tone, that I almost ignored the emotional weight of the question. After the words left her lips, she rested her hand on my knee for a moment.

I told her about *my pursuit of passion and purpose.*

I lived for so long without any clear thought about my own individuality, so I frantically tried to find my own meaning that would help mold an identity for myself. But the real pain came from distancing myself from who I really was, and instead, wore many masks that didn't fit my face.

This was partially catalyzed by my upbringing. I was raised by an overbearing and loving family, so I was showered with support and praise.

"But love, support, and care are all very important," Isabel interjected.

"They absolutely are," I said. "But the excessive praise I received— whether it was deserved or not— would inevitably lead me down one of two paths."

Isabel smiled. "And what were those paths?"

"Path A: I would remain in mediocrity waiting for something to happen in my life, because I was told I was special all throughout my childhood. I would have no desire to take action and forge a new path on my own."

"And Path B?"

"I would feel an overbearing responsibility to figure out why I was special and to own a personality that would make me seem 'special.'"

"And which path did you end up taking?"

"Well, my curiosity and crippling fear of uncertainty led me down the second path. I wanted to find out what made me so special."

Isabel made a 'U' shape with her lips. "*Uncertainty is psychologically unpleasant,*" she said in a calming tone. "You desperately wanted to figure out your purpose so you could better figure out who you were, and who you would eventually become."

She was right on the nose. While I could adopt the fact that the universe is on a razor-thin edge of stability that could be wiped out at any second by a Higgs Boson vacuum bubble, and that we don't hold a unique purpose in this universe because we emerged from the same mud and soil as lizards and rats, *that's not a very fun explanation.*

Instead, I pursued almost a dozen different occupations and passion projects in hopes that one of them would fulfill me. These pursuits started in my sophomore year of college, when I wanted to become a doctor, so I switched my major to pre-med and interned at an Alzheimer's disease research laboratory.

Then, I wanted to become a philanthropist, so I chartered a college organization where students could organize free basketball workshops for kids who attended schools with underfunded physical education programs.

Then, I wanted to become an entrepreneur, so I launched a tech company after I used the idea for an entrepreneurship class.

Then, I wanted to become a comedian, so I started performing standup and writing satirical blogs on a website I created.

Isabel was enthralled with my long list of pursuits

"Are there anymore?" Isabel asked.

I told her there were. My pursuits went beyond my college years. Pursuing medicine, running a charity, starting a company, performing stand-up, and writing satirical articles were only a few of the *many* other potential passions I pursued over the years.

I wanted to be a marketer, a salesman, an engineer, a podcaster, a fashion designer, and even a magician at one point. But all of them fizzled out. I lost interest in each of them when I hit roadblocks that made me retract instead of push through.

My first biology exam in college came back with a 52% smeared in red ink with a circle around it. The teacher left a note on the first page: 'This score is a bit concerning, come see me at office hours.'

My charity struggled to garner interest from schools, I was struggling to recruit volunteers, and my board started to lose faith in my leadership. My tech company failed to secure any sort of funding or gain any traction on the platform. In this time, I became mediocre at many skills, instead of just mastering a select few. I was a human Swiss army knife with dull blades.

"Why do you think your pursuits failed?" Isabel asked.

"I probably just had an immature mind— continuously lily-pad hopping from one interest to the next."

Isabel smiled. "That's part of the picture, but it's not the whole mosaic."

"What do you mean?"

She leaned back and decompressed her chest. "What do you think conventional wisdom would say about your failed passion pursuits?"

"I think conventional wisdom would say that I lacked the necessary grit and work ethic. I think they would say I just hadn't found my purpose yet, but one day, I would. I think they would say I'm too scatterbrained, and I need to focus on one thing."

"How was your work ethic as you pursued these passions?"

"Relentless," I told her. Not only was I looking for answers about life, but also for answers about success— and work ethic was more *recurrent* in the literature than anything else. The motivational "get shit done and stop caring what others think" speeches listed all over YouTube provided exemplary fervor for me, along with the thousands of other people uncertain with their lives and unhappy with themselves to take action and commit.

Every aspect of my life became about working harder than the person next to me— and to consistently stick with it. I romanticized sleep deprivation and constant hustling. I needed to work harder, smarter, and faster than everyone else.

I felt a wave of neo-liberalist zeal, like I had the urge to become someone like Bradley Cooper in *Limitless*. *That's a great idea— a fantastic fantasy!* Take a neurotropic, activate 100% of your brainpower, swindle millions in the stock market, and learn how to intelligently talk about the French Conquest of Algeria at a black-tie gala to impress people you never cared about in the first place.

Sounds like a plan! Here's your plaque for the 'Dumbest Daydream' award. Hang it somewhere nice where you can see it every day. Maybe above your toilet.

"That must have been unhealthy for your mind," Isabel pointed out.

And it was. I believed that the cure to my laziness was to flood myself with work, to become the hardest working person by never taking breaks.

I fiddled with the pop-up brush in my hands and looked up at the star-speckled sky. I saw Orion's Belt and the Three Sisters, all in line with each other as if they were all waiting at the post office.

I wonder what other planetary post offices are like?

Isabel hummed.

"Conventional wisdom would say you lacked a work ethic, but it seems like you had a *relentless* work ethic."

"It's always about work ethic or grit," I said. "Whether I didn't work hard enough, or I didn't work hard enough on the *right* things, or I didn't do the right *kind* of hard work."

Isabel stiffened her back. "But it's deeper than that," she responded. "Your reasoning for these failed pursuits aligns more with conventional wisdom than your specific situation. Lack of work ethic is a blanket answer used to throw over the fire. Starting a charity, running a tech company, and becoming a neurologist specializing in Alzheimer's research are all lofty goals on their own that come with an almost insatiable work ethic, but you already had this?"

"In a sense, I did."

Isabel smiled. We paused in silence while I continued to fiddle with the pop-up brush in my hands. The church bell rang once again.

Another hour had passed– at least, I thought so.

"Sammy," Isabel said. "You understood that chasing ordinary things will lead to ordinary results."

"I did."

"And you also understood that chasing extraordinary things with ordinary effort will lead to ordinary results?"

"Yes, I did."

"But now you don't understand *why*. You don't understand *why* you chased these passions in the first place. You said you wore masks that didn't fit your face. Why didn't they fit your face?"

"Because I failed at all of them."

Isabel frowned for a moment, then flashed a calm and soothing smile. "You may have failed in an objective sense, but why did they fail? You said you wanted to become a doctor, a philanthropist, an entrepreneur, a comedian, a marketer, a salesman, an engineer, a magician— these are all just *titles*. What happened as you adopted these *titles*?"

I thought in silence. I flipped through my list of passion pursuits on an imaginary Rolodex in my mind and noticed a pattern— *a recurrence*. That recurrence bubbling to the top of my mind was *my identity*.

Despite how my pre-med story wasn't uncommon, my academic and professional struggles weren't the reason why I quit — I quit because of *who I became.*

After declaring to my friends that I would pursue the path to becoming a physician, I instantly became smarter, harder-working, and more of a humanitarian in their eyes. This fed into my ego, making me pompous and full of myself. I saw other people pursue non-lucrative career paths and showed them pity instead of encouragement. I put myself atop a fictitious pedestal that made me seem more important than them.

When I ran my tech company, I had delusions of grandeur instead of hunger for Ramen Profitability. The majority of my time was spent building the website and designing app mockups.

I wasn't obsessed with the problem or my solution. I wasn't spending constant hours developing the product and doing usability tests with customers. I wasn't looking for a co-founder who shared the same values and complementary skills relative to mine. It felt better to show people a pristine website with prototype designs of the application, instead of telling people that I was talking with some teams when nothing had materialized yet.

When I ran my charity, instead of testing the concept out in a micro-setting or organizing the volunteering myself, I set up social media pages, made myself a founder on LinkedIn, and opened a checking account. These items are all important to have, but weren't necessary in the embryo stages of a charity. However, they were essential in reinforcing my philanthropic identity.

Even with my smaller passion pursuits, I could see this pattern. When I ran a clothing collective on campus, I focused on the design of the website and social media handles more than the actual goal and purpose of the collective. When I ran a business satire blog, I was more focused on website design and SEO instead of generating organic content.

This pattern became clear in my head. One by one, the reason for these failed pursuits became more apparent. The wave of anxiety returned. I started twirling my hair, knotting the strands together, and pulling them out. I caught myself after a few seconds and swatted my hand away from my hair. I popped out the hairbrush and started raking my hair back with the plastic bristles. After untying a few of the knots, I popped the hairbrush back in and took a deep breath. Now, I could give Isabel a true intrinsic answer.

"I associated these lofty goals with a certain identity . . . but the identity I was pursuing wasn't holistic. It wasn't who I was."

Isabel nodded for me to continue.

"During these audacious pursuits, I felt more of a serotonin kick from telling people about what I was doing instead of actually doing it. It was nice to tell people that I was starting a charity or a tech company, but it was awful to actually run it. Yet, it was a quick way to inflate my lifestyle and identity to my friends."

Isabel smiled. "So why did these pursuits fail, Sammy?"

"The pursuits didn't fail. *I failed.* I failed because I chased these passions, not to make something impactful, but to instead adopt the identity that came with it."

I had been gripping the pop-up brush in my right hand. I slowly released my grip and let it sit in my palm. I opened the lid and looked at the mirror— one of the small fractures had been repaired. Isabel looked at the mirror and smiled again.

"I think we've reached the source of the pain."

PERSONALITY

— *JOURNAL ENTRY 3* —

November 18, 2018

My friend from San Francisco visited town, so we decided to go out to a bar that night, despite my pure hatred for overpriced drinks and my lack of liquid intelligence to whip up a sub-par cocktail. But he wanted to take the edge off of paying $3,000 a month for an apartment the size of a woodshed, so taking shots of lidocaine to help him numb the pain was a justifiable reason for me to go. At the bar, I saw a girl I only somewhat knew from college, but still thought it would be nice to say hi. I approached her with a Cheshire cat grin and started talking with over-the-top artificial enthusiasm that even sounded downright cynical at one point. Undeniably, she called me out and pronounced that even after working in the entertainment industry for many years, my approach was the fakest she had ever received.

———————

I glazed my thumb over the mirror where the fracture had been mended. I looked for any hairline cracks in the area, and to see if there was any glue or putty inside of them. *Maybe part of the mirror had pushed itself back together while it was in my grip?*

I scratched my head. I thought I was going insane. Isabel watched me thoroughly inspect the mirror and smiled.

"You won't find the answers in there," she affirmed.

I looked up at her with a look of determination in my eyes. I went back to searching for the hairline cracks. Isabel gave me a gentle nudge.

"The mirror is still broken."

I grunted at her. "So, what does that mean? That this mirror will just magically fix itself? This must be some magic mirror, because normal mirrors don't just fix themselves."

I snapped the lid closed and waved the pop-up brush at her. "First, you start speaking proper English like a research paper, and now things just magically repair themselves? I get that this is probably some vivid dream, but it's getting a bit too *surreal*."

I retracted the mirror away from Isabel's face and held it in my hands. The lid remained shut. I looked over the large patch of farmland with the silhouette of the mountain range in the background. There was a wilting Mexican pine tree in the distance.

"Like, can I restore things now? Look at me, they call me Sam the Great Healer!" I announced with a royal flair. I started gesturing my hands out, stretching my wingspan. "I can heal anything I please!"

I looked at the wilting tree and made silly hand gestures toward it like I was casting a spell. The tree remained wilted, so my magical restoration powers failed. I was brought back to reality, *or whatever the hell this was*. Isabel remained calm throughout my ridiculous demonstration and simply smiled at me.

"Remember, Sammy, this mirror is more than just a mirror. *It's an artifact*. It's a physical representation of your pain. We've made progress, but we're not finished. You won't find any cracks in the silvering. The answers you're looking for are in your pains."

I thought more about *my identity* and less about my mystical powers of restoration. The pains I had related to it, not only with my passions. My pain came from what I pursued and how I pursued them, but also from who I was and who I expressed myself as to others. I told Isabel about what happened at the bar with my friend from San Francisco. She flashed me a smile.

"What went through your head after?" she asked.

"I immediately thought 'why the hell did you do that?' and 'why did you just pretend like she was one of your best friends?' Those were the first two thoughts that jolted into my cerebrum."

Cerebrum? Are you trying to be pseudo-intelligent again? Why not throw semi-liquid in there again?

"So, why did you do that?" Isabel asked.

"I'm not sure. I wanted to be nice and positive. I thought it would help me attract people."

But I didn't reveal how I also spent days thinking of all the witty comebacks I should have said to her while I was in the shower. My conditioner and body wash were there to back me up.

"And what was the outcome of blindly adopting this type of positivity?" Isabel asked.

"It didn't feel sincere or authentic. It didn't feel like who I really was. But it wasn't only positivity. I also blindly adopted gratitude."

Isabel smiled and nodded for me to elaborate. I told her how gratitude became a way for me to eschew negative feelings about certain situations in my life, and instead, blanket them with generic appreciation. Gratitude made me feel less terrible about things that were objectively terrible about my life. Instead of acknowledging the painful aspects of my life, I opted to instead think gratefully about things I did have. I wanted to feel more positive about the world, so that I could be more positive as a person.

But I came to realize that this was a byproduct of consulting external sources. To be positive and thankful were *recurring* antidotes that were recommended by these sources. To reduce the amount of friction or combative behavior with other people.

"I see," Isabel settled. "So, you understand the *recurrence*, but do you also understand the *damage*?"

"Not really," I told her. "I'm still lost."

"Take a shot at it."

"I'm— I'm not sure. I don—"

She interrupted, "I know you have a hunch, Sammy."

I fell silent. The only thing I knew was that it felt fabricated and against my own internal ethos, regardless if people weren't vigilant enough (like my "friend" at the bar) to call me out on it. Isabel started to hum, but I jumped back in with a quick conclusion. The swaying of the tall corn stalks in the distance caught her eye as she focused her attention back at me when I was ready to provide an answer.

I cleared my throat and sat up straight to fix my posture.

"The new principles I applied in my life also created ripple effects that impacted people around me."

Isabel looked intrigued and nodded for me to continue.

"I would integrate them into my life without understanding the effect they had on other parts of my life. I was doing something at the expense of another thing, or person, without even noticing it. My adoption of this over-the-top positivity and gratitude blinded my objective lens. I was hesitant to speak my mind to avoid offending someone, so people didn't take me seriously or treat me like an adult because I was too agreeable."

Isabel smiled. "That's a pretty good shot."

I gave her a grin back. "I also had to understand that I wouldn't always be kind, positive, and upbeat, because every so often, the entropic nature of reality would knock my damn teeth out."

Isabel flexed her lips toward her ears and brought her attention back to the corn stalks. "We've only scratched the surface. We need to dig deeper to the core."

"I thought I dug pretty deep."

"You did, but we can go further. Tell me what happened."

"About what?"

"Positive psychology. What happened when you adopted it?"

I told Isabel how I started to force myself to pretend to care about things. I would force myself to laugh at jokes that I didn't even find funny. I would pretend to be interested in everything that came out of someone's mouth. I would share trite, dilapidated information in hopes of sounding interesting. I would be grateful for things, hoping I would get some sort of newfound appreciation of the world around me.

Isabel hummed and went into what looked like meditative thought. I took this chance to gaze around the pueblo. The stark lining of the mountain range cut the sky and land in half, and a cold gust of wind flowed through the town square. Unlatched screens clinked against the shop windows while the tree branches danced in harmony. I sat there anxiously, but patient. I started twirling my hair, knotting the strands together, and pulling them out. Like clockwork, I swatted my hand away and popped open the hairbrush to rake my hair back.

Isabel finally mustered a response. My attention shifted away from the swaying, rustling trees and back onto Isabel.

"The *damage* here, Sammy," Isabel said, "is the external comparison."

"Well, duh," I bantered at her with a chuckle.

"You had partially understood the damage without knowing it. I listened to your attempts as I thought you had understood it."

"I guess I hadn't?"

"That's okay, Sammy. Over time, you will become more in tune with yourself and better at coming to these understandings."

"I see. So how did I understand without even knowing it?"

Isabel smiled. "How did you feel as a person when you adopted positive psychology?"

"It didn't feel honest."

"Right. You said it felt fabricated and against your own internal ethos."

"Positivity is great, but I prioritized it over honesty."

"Yes, that's true. And the crux we are trying to get to is why you adopted these traits. Do you remember telling me this?"

"I do. I wanted people to like me. I wanted to look nicer and more approachable."

"And is that intrinsic or extrinsic motivation?"

"Extrinsic. Positive psychology wasn't something that I fundamentally believed to be good, but because others did, I adopted the traits."

Isabel nodded, giving me the seal of approval that I understood the *damage*— sacrificing my true self for an extrinsic return. Because I didn't feel like myself, hyper-vigilant people like my friend at the bar were able to cut through my façade easily.

But I didn't feel complete here.

"How should I go about treating new people? How should I present myself to others? Which traits should I hold in high regard and which ones should I discard?" I asked.

"You already know the answer to those questions," Isabel implied with a smile.

"Yes, but is there a guiding principle I should follow? Is there a good one to reference to help give me a foundation of how to treat others?"

Isabel hummed, clasped her hands together, and rested them on her lap.

"Sammy," she said. "Before we can unearth those answers from yourself, we should address guiding principles. These are the roadblocks to your authenticity."

Isabel smiled and looked over the tall fields of corn stocks. I sat there in silence, preventing my hand from reaching for the hair on my scalp.

I opened the lid of the pop-up brush in my hand. Most of the mirror was still shattered, but the slice that was magically restored was still intact.

How do I activate my healing powers?

"We should get the blood in our legs flowing," Isabel said. I put the pop-up brush back in the box with the other artifacts and curled the box in my right hand. We got up from the white bench and walked away from the *pueblo*'s main plaza, back into the residential area.

Isabel took a sharp turn into a narrow alley and I followed like the loyal Labrador Retriever that I was. The paved road of the main plaza slowly transformed into dirt and rocks. I could hear the crunching and cracking of the dirt pressed against the bottom of my shoes with each step. Mounds of rocks and minerals were pushed to the side to clear the road for cars and carts pulled by mules. The alley was lined with the brick walls of homes and the wood-sticked gates of small patches of grass.

We walked past a mural painted on one of the few cement walls in the alley. It depicted children holding hands and running around in a circle on a patch of grass, like they were playing ring-around-the-rosie. A bright yellow sun with a smiley face was painted in the top right corner, with white puffy clouds scattered over the top. A caption was written on the bottom of the mural in bright blue letters.

Trata a Todas con Amabilidad

Treat Everyone with Kindness

I stopped in place and scoffed. Isabel, who was a few steps ahead of me, turned around and asked why I did that.

— 153 —

I pointed to the caption. "I don't agree with this," I announced like a politician giving a firm stance on a delicate topic. Isabel looked at the caption and smiled.

"You don't agree with this principle?"

"I don't."

Isabel hummed. "Why not?"

"I don't think this is a good principle for treating everyone. Like, treat *EVERYONE* with kindness? There are people in the world who I definitely don't think deserve kindness!"

Isabel nodded, but I could see on her face that she didn't agree with me.

"It reminds me of the Golden Rule," I told her.

"What's that?"

"*Treat others the way you want to be treated.* But despite what every summer camp and anti-bullying seminar held at my school's gymnasium wanted me to believe, the Golden Rule, in my opinion, was pretty damn fallible."

"How so?"

"Well, I really hate birthdays and don't want anyone to give me any presents or any form of celebration."

Isabel nodded. "Why do you dislike your birthday?"

"I genuinely hate the celebration and fanfare."

"It must be more than that."

There really wasn't. To me, birthdays feel like a participation trophy given to you by the world— celebrating your continuous breathing of oxygen on this planet that you made it another year. To some, birthdays are amazing, like a sarcoma patient who was told she wouldn't live past 29, then celebrating her 30th year on this planet. I can get behind that.

"So, what makes the Golden Rule fallible?" Isabel asked.

"There are so many people who love birthday celebrations and the accompanying guilt-free red velvet cake that comes with it, but the Golden Rule tells me to treat their birthdays as insignificant, because that's what I would like. I mean, I know I can be a mood-killer or a Debbie-downer at times, but I wouldn't let my beliefs ruin another person's celebration."

Isabel nodded. "I see. So, if this rule is fallible, why do so many people know and follow it?"

"Well, I think because it looks nice on the surface and it's easy to understand. But people have already grabbed their fire pokers and ripped holes in the validity of this rule, which led to the *Platinum Rule—treat others the way THEY want to be treated.*"

"That seems like a better alternative," Isabel said with a smile.

"But it's not," I replied, completely deflating Isabel's enthusiasm. "On the surface, it seems like an amazing alternative. But not everyone like me wants to be neglected on their birthday. So, the better rule is to treat others the way they want to be treated, since everyone is different and unique in their own way."

"Do you think that limits the Golden Rule?"

"I don't think so. What about the birthday-zillas? The people who demand everyone treat them like they're the ruler of an imaginary monarchy? What about addicts who prefer to live on a razor-thin edge of mortality instead of seeking treatment? What about the people who believe they deserve respect when they embody hatred and evil?"

"I see."

"And what about me?" I rhetorically asked with an antagonistic tone, hoping Isabel wouldn't actually reply with an answer. She didn't.

"I preferred to stay inside by myself for many years of my life because it was safer. I didn't have the skills to equip myself in a social setting. The Platinum Rule says *leave me to rot*— despite the fact that it was painfully obvious that what I was doing was unhealthy."

Isabel sat in silence and I cooled off. She looked at me and suggested I take a breath. I let the brisk air flow into my mouth, and the forest scent pervade my nostrils. Sometimes, you need to put a saddle on a mustang, especially if it's thrashing.

"You know the guiding principles you don't use," Isabel stated after I exhaled. "The Gold and Platinum Rule don't align with how you want to guide yourself as an individual. It's not something you want to equip to your identity. But what rule do you admire?"

I thought for a moment until nothing came up. I couldn't think of a rule or guiding principle off the top of my head, but something else came to my mind . . . or rather, someone else.

"I don't know of a rule," I said. "But I know of a person. My friend Michael."

Isabel hummed in interest. "Why him?"

I remember Michael from college. I only had a few interactions with him, but each one was enthralling to watch. Michael can be best described as an acquired taste, like whiskey or pineapple on pizza. He's loud, bombastic, and will give you a funny nickname within five minutes of meeting you. Clare is Clur, Benjamin is Benjo, and Maddy is the Antichrist (she was his ex-girlfriend who slashed his tires). Essentially, he's the human embodiment of a sour Warhead, so first impressions of Michael usually leave a dissatisfied aftertaste, like having a pill scrape your taste buds before going down your throat.

But spend enough time with Michael, and he becomes pleasant company. He will diligently incorporate you in conversations, just so that you won't feel left out. He will listen to your problems void of any cynicism or destructive criticism. He will position himself as a reliable friend. Michael doesn't treat people the way he wants to be treated, nor the way people want to be treated; he treats each person the way he feels they each *should* be treated. Instead of receiving the same exact interaction with Michael, each person gets their own unique piece of him like a jigsaw puzzle.

I described all of these things about Michael to Isabel, and she merely smiled.

"You don't have a rule," she stated.

I scratched my head. If I had a nickel for every time my face became visibly perplexed, I could have bought a small island in the British Virgin Islands by now.

"What do you mean?"

"Michael didn't believe in treating everyone one way or another. He didn't follow a rule, guideline, or principle. You admire his interactions because they're flexible and malleable."

I told Isabel that I understood my guiding principle. Sometimes, people don't know how to treat themselves the right way. Sometimes people don't know how to treat other people the right way. Sometimes, people need to hear things that won't sit well with them.

The way I treat people based on my internal ethos may not sit pleasantly with people at first. It takes time for people to get used to the behaviors and quirks of other people, but I'd rather have the dynamics of my relationships with people remain flexible instead of trying to fit nicely with others based on some static principle.

"The Graphene Rule," I replied. *"Treat others by your internal ethos and not by some static principle."*

Isabel looked content. "I think that sounds very authentic."

The church bell rang in the distance.

"Do you think you're missing something?" Isabel asked. At first, I didn't pay attention. I was counting the minutes back in my head to understand the true cadence of the church bell. I had a habit of getting lost in a single thought and burrowing as deep as I could into it to find the nucleus.

We continued to walk through the alleyway, the crunching and crackling of the dirt as it pressed against the bottom of my shoe. Isabel walked patiently with her hands behind her back. She reiterated her question to me.

"What do you mean?" I asked.

"The *Graphene Rule.* This anti-rule leaves out a key part that could use some more understanding."

"I'm still not sure what you're getting at."

"What do you think is the difference between people who prioritize authenticity and others who don't?"

"Authentic people probably go through more trouble and hardships."

"Why is that?"

"Because they don't try to mold themselves into a round peg to fit perfectly into a round hole."

"So how does that create more trouble and hardships?"

"Because they don't fuck around."

Isabel lifted an eyebrow, as if to say, *cut out the vulgar language*. But in a moment, she returned back to her jubilant, calm self and nodded for me to continue.

"Authentic people take their controversies to the chest instead of avoiding them. They relish the opportunities to give a piece of their mind and avoid playing Kabuki theater with the public."

"What kind of hardships will they go through?"

"Too much authenticity can be self-destructive. In most situations, people will only meet the surface layer of your identity, but people with unfiltered authenticity don't have that same layer."

Isabel hummed. "Our brain needs a screening mechanism for us to decide whether we want to continue engaging with a particular person."

I could understand this concept, but still I asked how this related to the Graphene rule. She explained how I needed to understand the function of *self-monitoring*, which was to be constantly aware of my surroundings and to understand (to a degree) what was appropriate and what wasn't.

This was easy enough for me to understand. I absolutely dread long meetings at work, but I'm not going to stand on my chair and shout "This is pointless!" just because of this.

"But there's another aspect to self-monitoring," Isabel explained. My ears perked up like a dingo hearing the footsteps of a nearby rabbit.

"You also need to perform and deliver to the best of your abilities, since no matter how much you pout and whine, other people will still judge you on the surface.

"So, I can't have this authentic attitude and be a poor performing person. Is that what you're saying?"

"Exactly. To think you can be yourself without any self-monitoring or ramifications that come with the lifestyle is dangerous. You need to back up your individuality."

"I see."

"So, we have now understood the personality traits that were damaging to your identity— adopting positive psychology in hopes of an extrinsic return. Now, we want to unearth the truly authentic personality traits that you hold in high regard and use them to build your foundation."

"And how would we do that?"

"What attributes do you value more than positivity?" Isabel asked.

"Well, there are a lot of attributes I care about. Empathy, support, hard work, responsibility."

"But what about the most important attributes? Which do you value the most?"

I didn't have to think of the answer. It came naturally. I told Isabel what I valued the most: *honesty and humor.* She smiled.

"I understand the dichotomy between blanket positivity and honesty, but why humor?"

I told Isabel about my time at Brookstone, my comedic bits, and my experience with Glen. She nodded.

"But why do you use humor specifically? That's a nice story, but we want to understand why you value humor over all other characteristics?"

"Because, over time, my humor evolved into a defense mechanism— which goes hand-in-hand with improving my confidence. I always try to find a way to make fun of something in a self-deprecating, deadpan kind of way. If I could lacerate myself with jokes before someone else could, I'd have the upper hand and wouldn't feel so insecure about myself. Even with all the things that I truly don't like or even downright hate about myself, spinning it in some humorous way made it less desirable to criticize. Nobody wants to stab you when you already have a fresh knife wound in your stomach, especially when you've been making them belly laugh for 30 straight minutes."

"It seems like honesty and humor should be the foundation you mold your personality around. But you didn't."

"I didn't, because honesty and humor overlap with bluntness and discomfort. Some people are taken aback by people with no filter, and others with a different sense of humor may get offended. My humor and honesty eventually became suppressed as I got older, since I thought I would offend or tarnish relationships with people. I've felt the need to tread carefully, since it's almost become a crime to make a controversial joke or statement nowadays. I would restrain myself in order to create a contrived aura of politeness in social and professional settings. I reserved myself to not satirize others, but as we know, this wasn't authentic."

Isabel smiled. "Honesty and humor are your foundational characteristics, but they aren't the only ones. You're also kind, empathetic, supportive, hardworking, and attentive. But those are guided by the foundational characteristics you decided to suppress."

"Exactly, because I was afraid of pissing people off."

Isabel smiled. The alley finally opened up to two other streets. The first street was lined with the same brick walls and the second was lined with tall cacti and vegetation. Isabel took a turn into the second street and I followed, clutching the box in my right hand. The street was directly in line with the silhouette of the mountain range in the distance. It looked as if we could walk directly into the mountain if we kept going straight. Isabel hummed and turned to me in stride.

"I don't think you're afraid of pissing people off."

I could still hear the crunching and crackling of the dirt pressed against the bottom of my shoes. I was taken aback by her statement.

"What do you mean?"

"I think you're afraid of pissing off the wrong people. What you should be more aware of is *pissing off the right people*."

Again, I scratched my head. Why would I want to piss anyone off? Why create unnecessary animosity?

"Self-monitoring," Isabel said, "can help you avoid pissing off the wrong people. Your authentic personality traits, like humor and honesty, can help you piss off the *right* people."

"But who are the right people?"

Isabel smiled. "The people who conflict with your fundamental beliefs. The people who gawk at your radical ideas. The people who uphold an outdated monolith that you believe needs revising."

"I see."

"But this is a tricky road to take. Some people fall and perish, while others flourish. Many people have radical ideas, but very few see the fruits of their labor. Do you know why?"

I gulped, knowing the answer that was about to come.

"Because they didn't piss off the wrong people?"

"Yes, exactly."

"But who are the *wrong* people, then?"

"The people who were with them in the first place. The people who were catalyzed and taken by their ideas. The people who were supported by these figures when they started."

I was silent for a moment. Isabel opened a new door in my head for me to peer through. As a kid, I would sleuth my way around the house so I could watch *South Park* on television. It quickly became my favorite show, not only for its dark humor and honesty, but also because it was forbidden in my house. My parents wouldn't let me watch it, which made the show more desirable.

South Park was content with pissing off the right people: Kanye West, Sean Penn, Sarah Jessica Parker, Michael Moore, The

Parents Television Council, Paramount Studios, the Catholic League, the Church of Scientology, the Motion Picture Association of America, and the *entire* country of China, but not independent filmmakers and their loyal fan base. They stuck to their guns, never apologized for their criticism and satire, and always made sure to provide an entertaining, well-written, compelling, and absolutely hilarious episode for their fans.

I also thought about Allen Iverson and Marc Benioff. Iverson was content with pissing off the NBA when he wore baggy jeans, flashy chains, medallions, snapbacks, and XXL t-shirts to games, but not the players who stood by him in the fight to dress authentically. Benioff was content with pissing off their larger and stronger competitor, Siebel Systems, when Salesforce was still in its infancy, but not his employees and customers, who were the key drivers in his company's success.

We kept walking down the street sprawling with vegetation, but the mountains looked even further away now.

Was this an optical illusion?

After a few moments of walking in silence and hearing only the wind blow through the trees and the crunching and cracking of the dirt, Isabel asked about my time at Brookstone and why I was content with pissing off Glen.

"Because Glen was against what I believed," I told her, "which was that you could use humor to win customers and enjoy a dead-end job. I was content with pissing off Glen when it came to adapting to the new circumstances of my life, even though it could have gotten me fired. I held my values to higher strata."

"And who did you avoid pissing off?"

"My coworkers. I had a great rapport with them during the slow hours of the day, and they would support me if I were blamed for anything that threatened my employment. They also supported and even sometimes laughed at my humorous bits on the sales floor."

Isabel smiled. "We now understand why you hold honesty in high regard by examining the *Graphene Rule*, but we haven't yet understood why you do the same with humor. We know that you use humor as a defense mechanism to improve your self-confidence, but humor isn't the only mechanism you can use to achieve those outcomes. Why do you think you choose to use humor?"

"Because humor is something that's fundamental to my core identity."

Isabel nodded and kept walking in silence for a moment. I thought about my humor, which was the side of me I hid for so long without understanding the broader implications. I eventually decided to stop caring.

I make jokes to make people laugh— and even sometimes offend– but never to hurt someone. I don't believe anyone based on their sex, race, religion, or any other characteristic is allowed to have this impenetrable force field that is invincible to criticism or humor. Humor brought everyone to an equal playing field, even myself.

But humor has also given me a wider peripheral vision of events that happened to me. Humor has helped me focus less on *what is said* and more on *how and why it was said*. It has helped me understand *intent* and *context*, both of which can be more dangerous than the words themselves. I think the knife is less dangerous than the man wielding the knife, and I think the man wielding the knife in his kitchen to cut carrots is less dangerous than the man wielding the knife to rob someone in a back alley.

Isabel finally broke the silence.

"What if someone doesn't think your joke is funny?"

"I've already accepted that," I told her. "I can't change how people perceive my jokes, but I'm willing to take that risk and fight against unnecessary ramifications from people who feel attacked, because I know my jokes never come from a place of hatred. Rather, they come from a place of *honesty*."

"I see."

"I understand that the outraged few are more vocal than the satisfied many, but humor is an authentic piece of myself, and I wouldn't suppress it any longer— even if it means pissing people off."

Isabel smiled. "You're making great progress, Sammy."

I smiled back and gazed over at the mountain range, now even further from us, when the clicking sound came from inside the box.

I opened the lid, took all the artifacts out, and placed them on the ground. I dug my face into the box to see where the noise could have come from. Isabel watched me and smiled.

"The mirror, Sammy."

I took my face out of the box. I grabbed the pencil and the chain link and put them back in the box. I shut the lid and gripped the box in my armpit. I picked up the pop-up brush and opened the lid. Another fracture had been repaired. I could see most of my face in the reflection.

The wind still threw gentle gusts through the *pueblo*, picking up the scattered leaves on the dirt roads. The church bell rang again.

How much time had passed since I had woken up?

MENTAL HEALTH

— JOURNAL ENTRY 13 —

January 20, 2019

When I was around 12 or 13 years old, my parents sent me to a Jewish sleepaway camp where I cried every night because I was homesick. It took four straight days for me to convince my camp counselor to let me talk to my mother on the phone. I took my ADHD medicine every morning, despite the absence of assignments and tests at camp.

Again, the medicine inhibited my appetite, so I skipped lunch and opted for the 10 pm PB&J sandwiches the camp left out for me and the other medicated kids with abnormal eating schedules.

One night, a counselor escorted me back to the cabin as I held a double-decker PB&J sandwich on a plate. Riley, one of the campers complained.

"Why does Sam get food at night?" he whined from his bunk.

Riley was mad because his stomach was still growling. The kosher Brisket and mashed potatoes didn't subside his hunger, but then again, he was pretty bulky for a 10-year-old. The rest of us were twigs tied together with a layer of skin. Riley tried to convince us that his excess blubber was actually muscle from all the pushups he would do with his brother in their garage, but his bed springs told a different story.

I walked in the cabin with my head down to avoid eye contact and ate my sandwiches under the covers so no one could see me. Riley kept howling and whining to the counselor.

"How did you deal with all that hatred you had inside of you when you came to America?" I asked.

Isabel ignored my question as if she couldn't answer it. She raised an eyebrow at me for a moment, before, as always, returning to her pleasant aura.

We kept walking and I curled the box with my right hand. The wind kept rustling the vegetation all around us. The houses started to fade away from the sides of the street and were replaced with farmland and vegetation.

We weren't in the *pueblo* anymore. We were walking through the outskirts and still toward the mountain, but it kept moving further from us with every step we took. It was much darker than the *pueblo*, but the moonlight provided ample light for us to see as much as we needed.

Isabel broke the silence. "We're getting closer."

I continued to look at my semi-complete reflection in the mirror. There was still a large fracture that ran from the top down, toward the right side of the mirror. If you focused long enough on it, it formed a crude outline of the shape of California.

"But we're still not finished," Isabel added. I closed the lid of the pop-up brush and put it inside the box. Isabel asked what else needed to be addressed about my *identity*. I didn't have an answer. I started twirling my hair, knotting the strands together, and pulling them out. Isabel watched me do this longer than any of the previous times. She looked intrigued.

"Why do you do that with your hair?" she asked.

"It's a compulsive disorder," I told her as I opened the pop-up brush and raked my hair back. She furrowed her brow.

"Why don't you try stop doing it?"

"It's not that easy," I said.

I dealt with ADHD, anxiety, and phases of depression for many years. For a moment, it sounded trite.

Is there anyone in the world that hasn't dealt with any of these mental illnesses? I didn't have another way to categorize them, and *mental illnesses* seemed off-putting.

My first diagnosis for ADHD was at the age of 10. I left the psychiatrist's office with a bottle of pills. Prescription medicine was the safe, most common route to cure, or at least subside, my mental illness, so I never looked at any other avenues. But over time, I started to notice a pattern of behavior that I thought was unusual.

Isabel hummed and we continued to walk in a moment of silence. I gazed at the silhouette of the mountain range in the distance.

"Do you feel like these traits about you are permanent?" she asked.

"For a long time, I did," I told her. "Personality traits seemed more fluid, and mental illnesses felt more unchangeable. It was easy to adopt positive psychology, but hard to reduce my anxiety. It was easy to become hardworking and gritty, but hard to pull myself out of depression. My mental health is a fundamental part of my identity, and I want to better understand it than I already do."

Isabel asked about my ADHD.

"I was told I had a chemical imbalance in my brain with no control over fixing it," I said. So, I turned to medication for mediation. I walked into the psychiatrist's office with focus issues, and left with a mental illness and a prescription for Ritalin. The medication treated my behavior without addressing my environment, social skills, or any other multivariate factors that could have contributed to my hyperactivity and lack of focus.

Looking back when I was told that I had ADHD, it felt more like a judgment of a narrative instead of a diagnosis based on pathology. I was 10 years old and was forced to sit in a metal chair for eight hours—*how do you expect any kid to focus?*

"And how did that feel?" Isabel asked.

"Like a *compromise*. The psychiatrist just said, 'hey, you have this disease we can't cure, but if you take this pill every day, we can mitigate these behaviors that other people don't like.' It wasn't an ideal solution."

"But what about your anxiety and depression? You were never formally diagnosed."

"I was prescribed pills, but never took them. I've already dealt with enough side effects from the ADHD medication."

Isabel hummed in interest. "What were those side effects?"

"The pills I took for eight years were a huge benefit for me academically, but I still suffered socially, physically, and neurologically. The medication inhibited my appetite, so I lost substantial weight. It led to a compulsive disorder, contributed to my phases of loneliness, and created a loss of joy and happiness."

Isabel smiled without teeth. "You have a very holistic understanding of your mental health," she said. "So, what are you struggling with?"

"I'm struggling with how to guide myself moving forward. How do I better mitigate these aspects of my mental health? They're part of my *identity*, but I don't believe they're immutable illnesses that have to be moderated with medication."

Isabel closed her eyes and went into some form of meditation while we walked. I glanced over at the vast farmland springing with flowers, trees, and corn stalks. The fresh vegetation and a scent in the air rekindled an old memory.

"Sammy," Isabel said as she returned from her meditative thought. "Let's identify the *recurrence* and the *damage*. What do you think the *recurrence is*?"

"Wouldn't it be the mental illnesses themselves?"

"Not entirely. These are all an effect of the *recurrence*."

"I see."

"What about the way you perceived your mental illnesses?

"Well, I saw them as immutable characteristics."

"Right, so when you were diagnosed with an illness that seemed immutable, how did that change your perception of your behaviors?"

I thought for a moment and reflected on the times that my mental illnesses got in the way: the thousands of days I spent experimenting and taking different medications; the situations I avoided because they made me feel unpleasant. But as I thought further, I started to notice a pattern in how I treated my mental illnesses and how they molded and shaped who I was.

They were frequently just being used as *excuses*.

"I established the presupposition that the problems in my life were due to anxiety, depression, and ADHD. These illnesses felt like immutable characteristics I would have to live with."

She nodded for me to continue.

"I attributed my nervousness in large social groups and my panic attacks in stressful situations to anxiety. I attributed my feeling of loneliness, sadness, lack of self-worth, and fulfillment to depression. I attributed my lack of grit with passion projects and my lack of focus in school to my ADHD. I blamed my ADHD for not listening to people when they talked. I blamed my anxiety for blowing up over small inconveniences. I blamed my depression for continuously canceling plans with friends, since I just wanted to sit home by myself."

Isabel smiled. "That's the *recurrence!*" she exclaimed.

I smiled back at her. We finally approached another connecting street. Isabel made the turn and I followed. We were no longer walking toward the mountains.

Isabel continued. "Now, we want to know the *damage* from the *recurrence.*"

"I would think that *blaming* my mental illnesses for certain behavior is the damage?"

"Not entirely– it's still an effect from the *recurrence*."

I paused and thought for a moment, trying to solve this mental Rubik's Cube. She asked if I thought I had control over these illnesses. I told her I didn't. She hummed and decompressed her chest with a long exhale.

"Let's dig deeper into this," she said. When we are diagnosed with an illness that we have no control over fixing or curing, what do we do?"

"We get treatment."

"Yes, and your treatment was medication."

"Right."

"But your medication wasn't working."

"Well, it was working, since it made me more focused."

"Yes, but the medication made you suffer socially, physically, and neurologically."

"Yes, it did."

"But you also talked about the environment you were in when you were diagnosed, and ultimately, prescribed medication. You were just a child sitting in a metal chair for eight hours to learn about subjects that you weren't really interested in."

"Yes, that's right." For a moment, I felt like a cheap animatronic that was programmed to say only a handful of phrases.

"Sammy," Isabel said in a softer tone. "Do you think your mental illnesses are the sole cause of your unwanted behavior?"

"What do you mean?"

"Would you agree that, sometimes, illnesses cause unwanted behavior?"

"Yes, I would."

"And how is unwanted behavior usually classified?

"I would say wrong, unpleasant, or even strange. Someone who constantly interrupts people while they talk is classified as wrong and unpleasant, while someone who gets so anxious in crowds that they pull out their hair is classified as *strange*."

Isabel explained to me how unwanted behaviors can be a side-effect of a pain that goes even deeper. Some of these pains we can understand, control, mitigate, and even sometimes, cure. With others, we can't do much about them.

I was taken aback, so I asked her to clarify. She beveled her cheeks and gave me a pleasant look.

"Do you think people with leukemia should apologize just because they can't donate blood?" she asked.

"No, I don't think so."

"Do you think people with sickle cell anemia should apologize for their constant fatigue?"

"No, I don't."

"Why shouldn't they?"

"Because they have diseases that they can't control themselves. Sickle cell anemia is caused by a gene mutation, and leukemia is caused by the uncontrollable growth of blood cells. Yes, we can practice prevention to an extent, but once we're diagnosed, there's nothing in our own willpower to cure ourselves of these diseases."

Isabel nodded. "These are the pains we don't have control over, but you felt the same way about your mental illnesses?"

"I did for a long time, because I saw my illnesses as immutable parts of myself. I frequently used them as excuses for my actions."

"Do you still think they're immutable?"

"Not in the same sense as sickle cell anemia or leukemia—diseases with clear cut pathologies."

Isabel smiled. "Do you think you still have ADHD?"

"I wouldn't say for a fact. I think it's fair to say that I've become quite adaptable to it. Yes, I get distracted all the time, but I think my environment, one with everything at my fingertips providing me an inundation of content and a flood of notifications, has been its own contribution to this. As I got older, I realized that creating a form of structure for myself, aligned with activities that interested me, could keep my attention in check."

"And what about your anxiety and depression?"

"I'm still working on it. For now, I'm trying to understand what aspects of my life ignite these feelings of anxiety and depressive states."

"So, how do your mental illnesses differ from the bodily disorders we talked about?"

"My mental illnesses aren't caused by a malfunction of my body. They're a mixture of genetic and environmental factors. Understanding my environment and behaviors can ease my ADHD, anxiety, and depression. Changing my behaviors or environment won't *cure* me of any bodily disorders, just like how moving to Ecuador to live on the warm and sandy beaches of the Galápagos Islands won't relieve me of my leukemia, and quitting a stressful job with an abusive manager won't relieve me of my sickle cell anemia."

Isabel grinned. "Do you see the *damage*?"

"I do. I called myself *diseased* so I didn't work to mitigate my behavior with new habits or a change in my environment. I saw these characteristics as immutable, so I denied myself responsibility."

Isabel crinkled her eyes. A brief silence carried over the conversation. Another click came from inside the box. I opened the lid and took out the pop-up brush. The layer of dirt had been wiped away and the bright blue shade of its shell popped in the moonlight.

I opened the lid and gasped.

The mirror was completely intact. No fractures, scratches, or hairline cracks. I could finally see my full reflection, but a new thought entered my head.

"Why did you decide to help me?" I asked.

She ignored my question yet again and gazed over the vast farmland. The tall corn stocks swayed back and forth from the gentle nudges of the wind.

I asked again. She relaxed and rubbed her hand on my back.

"I didn't decide to help you, my Sammy. *You* did."

I still had a blatant look of puzzlement on my face. She smiled without teeth. We kept walking in the moonlight. I slipped into what felt like unconsciousness.

Chapter 7

We weren't walking on a dirt road anymore. I no longer heard the crunching and crackling of the dirt pressed against the bottom of my shoes. The vegetation and vast acres of farmland on the sides were replaced with shops painted in pastel shades of orange, green, and yellow.

We had walked all the way to Mitla, 20 kilometers away from the *pueblo*. While it was supposedly a three-hour walk, my legs still didn't feel sore. My muscles weren't energized or restless, they just existed as if they were mechanical, doing all the walking for me while I filled my lungs with the same air that rustled the branches of the trees.

During the day, Mitla overflowed with tourists who purchased Aztecan souvenirs and authentically woven sweaters, scarfs, and carpets. Kids would run through the streets playing with toy guns and wooden dolls while their parents mingled with each other.

Now, in the dead of the night, the shop entrances were closed down with rusted brown gates. Again, not a single sound of footsteps, distance chatter, or the engine of a nearby car. The only sound came from the wind that blew through the branches, causing the leaves to rustle and fall to the ground.

Isabel found a wooden bench to sit on. I joined so I could rest my mechanical legs. I placed the box to my side and looked at my new view. The mountain range and long stretches of farmland was replaced by the Palace of Mitla.

Mitla is the most important archeological site of Zapotec culture, as many of the remains were still intact. The outer walls of the Palace were scribbled with zig-zags, spirals, and other geometric patterned designs.

Since we fully restored the mirror, Isabel didn't utter a word. We sat in silence, looking at the patterned designs on the outer walls of the palace.

I got anxious again, so I started twirling my hair, knotting the strands together, and pulling them out. I caught myself after a few seconds and swatted my hand away. I grabbed the pop-up brush out of the box and raked my hair back. I glanced back at the box, where the silver chain link and the pencil with its broken tip was still sitting inside.

I was most interested in the chain link, since it had no imperfections. The pencil had a broken tip and the pop-up brush had a shattered mirror.

However, the chain link was in perfect condition. I placed the pop-up brush back in the box and took out the chain link. I held it in my hand, looking at the silver finish glisten in the reflection of the moonlight.

Isabel finally spoke up. "It seems like you're ready to understand the next pain."

I looked blankly at the chain link.

What was there to fix? I inspected the surface to see if I could find any clues, marks, or hidden messages. I found none. Isabel smiled.

"You won't understand the *artifact* just by looking at it."

She let out a faint chuckle, but I wasn't amused. I had a habit of over-analyzing the painfully obvious. Everything was a puzzle to me, and I'd always exert as much brain power as I could to solve it, but the chain link stumped me.

"I don't understand," I admitted. "There's nothing about this chain link to examine– there are no clues. The pop-up brush had the shattered mirror, and the pencil had a broken tip, but this chain link is in perfect condition."

Isabel nodded and flashed a smile without showing her teeth.

"Sometimes, pain isn't physically apparent. Like the Mandarin, sometimes it's *absent*. It's in there for a reason, Sammy. But remember, you put the chain link in the box and only you can truly understand it."

I sat and meditated to myself, thinking what this chain link could represent.

What pain was it trying to tell me? We had already talked about so much. My passions, my personality, my mental health, my rule for treating others. Then I stopped in thought.

Others.

I thought about that mural– the children holding hands and running around in a circle. The caption at the bottom wasn't the only thing that irritated me.

"That mural," I told Isabel. "It made me feel different."

Isabel looked away from the palace and then back to me. I could see genuine interest in her eyes. "You looked at it more than I would imagine anyone else would." She smiled and added, "Why did you look at it for so long?"

"Well, the caption caught my attention."

"Yes, but there's more than that. What else?"

"The *others*. The *kids*. The ones holding hands and playing ring-around-the-rosie."

"What about them, Sammy?"

"Some were smiling, others were laughing. They all looked so happy playing with each other. They were obviously painted as friends. It made me feel how I've felt for so many years."

Isabel nodded "Made you feel what, Sammy?"

I exhaled and pressed my back against the bench. "Isolated."

— JOURNAL ENTRY 19 —

March 3, 2019

Throughout middle school, I carried around a blue binder filled with my assignments and notes.

That thing was my prized possession. I never went anywhere without it. It was with me so much, that some of my classmates started to notice. One day, when I went to use the bathroom after class, one of the kids took my binder and hid it behind the teacher's desk. I came back and turned (almost the) entire classroom upside down. I couldn't find my binder.

I went home that day and my body stayed in paraphyletic shock, worrying about not being able to finish my homework for the night. I had always completed my homework the night before, or on the bitter cold school bus ride in the morning.

But that night, I didn't. And I couldn't sleep. I picked the skin off my lip the entire night.

The next day, it was sitting at my seat in the same classroom. I picked it up and the kid who hid it laughed it off.

This isn't even a story about bullying. I wasn't the weird kid who said weird shit in class. I wasn't a target for bullying, nor was there very much to begin with at my school.

I was the kid who filled the class picture. I was the kid who was pretty much forgotten about in conversations ("Sam . . .? You mean Sam Rice? Wait, no, not that one. Which one is he again?")

What was so weird about this interaction was that I'd never spoken to this kid before, and he decided to take my binder and hide it, not knowing how much of a shitshow I would turn into because of that. What a strange thing to happen.

Then, I thought, would a future friend of mine do something like this to me? How do you let people into your life when you don't know what they're going to do to you?

FRIENDSHIP

We had talked in-depth about how my ADHD affected my personality, but it also played a huge role in my isolation. I also couldn't declare that it was the main ingredient, since my father was also reserved. Thus, genetics probably took a turn at stirring the cauldron. I spent many years in isolation, alone, with my thoughts and vices, devoid of friendships for many years to come.

"Did you attempt to make friends?" Isabel asked.

"All the time."

"But that's not unordinary."

"It wasn't. I was a teenager. We're all trying to fit in. I first thought that the problem was my shyness and quiet demeanor. One of my first stabs at forming friendships was for people to believe I was smart and interesting by becoming the loudest."

"Did that work?"

"Not at all," I chuckled.

Isabel nodded and smiled. "How else did you attract friends?"

"I would blindly do nice things for people."

"Like what?"

"I would drive people across town, because they didn't have a driver's license. I would get people tickets to basketball games so they could hang out with me, and hopefully from there, create a connection. I would give generic gifts to people who weren't my friends, but wanted them to be. For a while, I honestly didn't care, because I wanted to be around people and not be at home by myself in isolation."

Isabel nodded again. "Your strategy was blind altruism."

"Pretty much. My answer to not having friends was to become a doormat— thinking I could do favors for people, regardless if they conflicted with what I felt was right in my gut. But most people at this age wouldn't understand the difference, since, to them, I just seemed like a really nice person."

"Did any friendships come from these behaviors?

"I wouldn't say so. Pretending to be smart and interesting were both very short-lived facades. My blind altruism lasted longer, since people were more attracted to it. It was also harder for them to see the inauthenticity upfront."

"But what about now? Do you have friends?"

"Of course I have friends now, from different places, experiences, and times in my life."

"So, what are you struggling with now? What's the pain keeping you so miserable?"

"I still feel so alone."

Isabel rubbed my back with her hand. I held the glistening chain link in my hand.

I squinted my eyes at it, hoping some sort of drawing or clue would appear. I saw nothing.

———————

— *JOURNAL ENTRY 22* —

March 24, 2019

Forgive me for this journal entry, as this isn't about an experience from the past. It's about a feeling I've had.

I feel like this feeling feels important to write down (say the word "feel" one more time, I dare you). Its significance is important. Or at least, it feels important (you son of a bitch).

So, why not write about it? It goes against what my friend advised me to do, but then again, I'm no closer to fixing my pains than when I started. Full steam ahead.

When I was out with friends, I would have crippling panic attacks about not working on something and then had trouble actually enjoying myself in the present moment. Back at home, while working on something I felt like I should be working on (rather than me actually wanting to work on it), I would have crippling panic attacks about not having friends or anyone I could turn to.

Regularly, the panic attacks from working would triumph and I would occupy my time by working on something trivial, like designing an app screen that looked nice but would never get made, rather than going out with friends.

I was trying to do everything by myself and alienated a lot of my friends in the process. I didn't spend time with them, nor did I continue to create memories with them that we could laugh about 20 years from that point. I got invited to fewer events, trips, activities, weekend trips, late-night food runs, and everything else. I probably missed out on some really cool friendships and experiences because of this.

It's a choice I deeply regret to this day.

VICES

"You felt alone," Isabel exclaimed. "What did you do when you felt alone?"

"I would try to fill the void," I told her. "The easiest way was to play video games nonstop. I would play for three to four hours on weekdays and eight to nine hours on the weekends. Actually, now that I think of it, I probably played for even longer."

"What kind of games did you like?

"Strategy and first-person shooters were the ones I loved the most. If it involved killing a herd of orcs or wielding the entire army of Carthage, I was hooked. Then, there were the first-person shooters.

Halo, Call of Duty, I pretty much had all the weapons memorized. I remember going to a gun range years later with a friend of mine and was able to point out a FN-P90 and a M4 carbine hanging on the wall. The gun shop owner could clearly tell I played too many video games as a kid."

"I see."

"I also had a brief stint playing *Roller Coaster Tycoon*, but I don't tell my friends that."

Isabel chuckled. "And do you still play video games?"

"Much less now than before. Most of my time became used by YouTube as it grew in popularity. That's when I was inundated with external sources about living."

Isabel hummed. "When we want to find the specific pains that you fundamentally held before external sources, we looked at two aspects."

"Yes— *damage and recurrence.*"

"And we can see the damage, Sammy. But do you see the recurrence?"

"I'm not sure what you mean? The *recurrence* is isolation."

"It's deeper than that. Isolation is an effect, not the cause."

I tried to figure out what Isabel was referring to, but it was lost to me. My brain was puzzled, yet again.

"Were you destined to be alone by nature, or did you feel isolated by choice?" Isabel asked.

"I would hope it's not destined by nature."

"So, it's by choice?"

"I'm not sure. I think my actions have clearly made their own contributions. I chased passions that pushed me away from people. I had vices that kept me secluded. I didn't feel like I had people who I could rely on or go to for support. I didn't feel like a part of *any* community."

She let out a small chuckle and rubbed her hand on my back.

"Sammy, you found the *recurrence*!"

I furrowed my brow. "I don't think I get it, Isabel," I whispered in a deflated tone.

Isabel smiled, but this time, she flashed her teeth.

"You felt like you couldn't turn to anyone for support or help. You felt like you had to venture on this path alone."

"Yes, that's true."

"You couldn't chase these pursuits with other people, because you felt like you couldn't rely on them."

"I would agree with that, yeah."

"But you could turn to video games and external sources. You could rely on both of these outlets. Why is that?"

"I'm not sure."

"You could turn to them because of the *recurrence*."

"But what's the recurrence?"

Isabel smiled with comfort. "The recurrence, Sammy. The recurrence is *trust*."

As the words left her lips, a booming noise from the church bell erupted through the air. It was the top of the hour, but I wasn't sure which hour.

Trust. I didn't trust the cadence of the church bell.

TRUST

"The fracture," said Isabel. "The dismantling of your trust with friends started very early— *your blind altruism.*"

"What about it?"

"Did these same friends ever drive you around wherever you needed to go? Did they ever take you to basketball games? Did they ever give you gifts in return for the ones you gave? *Did they ever return any of your favors?*"

"No, nor should have I expected them to."

"Right, but at the time, you did. And they didn't. Your actions weren't reciprocated, and those friendships never materialized. Why do you think that is?"

"Because those friendships weren't authentic. They weren't built on mutual interests, fond memories, or any other tenant of a pure relationship."

"Yes, Sammy, I would agree with you. These unreciprocated and inauthentic friendships you had in the larva stages of your social life created a loss of trust with many of the new friends you would eventually make."

Again, Isabel catalyzed more self-reflection. Despite having these great friendships now, I blamed isolation as my pain instead of my lack of trust and openness. I would avoid investing my time and attention into other people, because I assumed that they were friends with me for something that I had. I would get combative with friends in my head when they asked me if I could drive them somewhere, or if they asked me for certain favors.

I didn't trust anyone. And because I didn't trust them, I couldn't be comfortable with them. I noticed a routinely cyclical process that would play out in social situations that would lead to my own detriment.

Something small would happen, whether I made an off-colored joke, or I said or did something stupid, and I'd then adopt the damaging mentality that everyone hated me. These thoughts brewing in my head quickly translated to my facial expressions and body language. I became unapproachable, and people wouldn't want to talk with me. This reduced the likelihood of forming true friendships and pushed me further into isolation. I didn't have my trusty 8x11 inch paper and black ballpoint pen with me, so I had to describe the cycle to Isabel.

Adopting The Mentality That Everyone Hates Me

Making Myself Appear Unapproachable

Not Forming Deep Connections With Others

Pushing Myself Further Into Isolation

"Why didn't you enlist anyone else to pursue any of your passion projects?" Isabel asked.

"I felt like there wasn't anyone I could rely on or truly trust. I didn't build a network of people who could support me, despite how many of my passions were pursued out of identity adoption. I thought I could work tirelessly to supplement the lack of teamwork I had, but I was painfully wrong. I frequently burned out, gave up, and picked large clumps of hair out of my scalp from stress."

Isabel smiled at my self-reflection. "But it's not only your lack of trust, Sammy," she said. "That's not the *recurrence*."

"It's not?"

"No, it's more than just trust. It's also what you trusted."

I gave a perplexed look. "What do you mean?"

"Your vices. You trusted video games and YouTube. When you felt alone, you occupied your time with both of these vices. They didn't make you feel alone anymore."

"Right. Video games sparked me as a hobby, but it was easy to indulge because I didn't need a second person to play. I gravitated towards video games because I could play at any time. It's hard to play tennis when no one is on the other side of the net to return the volley."

Isabel looked pleased "Would you still call it a hobby?"

"I wouldn't. I didn't have any alternative forms of pleasure in my life, so I settled for playing video games. But it was hard to quit, take breaks, or do anything else that would give me the same level of satisfaction."

I was also fighting a gladiator match against dopamine and I was holding a foam sword. The cards were stacked against me before they were even shuffled.

"So, video games became a dependency?" Isabel asked.

"I wouldn't call it a dependency. I would call it filling the void of human companionship."

When those words came out of my mouth, I immediately thought about my conversation with Martin on the way to the airport. I was moderating my video game use with friction, but the thing I was moderating wasn't video games— *it was isolation.*

"Every time you booted up your computer or console to play, would it load without fail?" Isabel asked.

"Yes, it did."

"Even if you wanted to play at four in the afternoon or four in the morning?"

"Yes, it would still load without fail."

"People can't always be with you 24/7, but a video game can."

"That made it more desirable," I added.

"Yes," Isabel agreed. "It was reliable. It would always turn on. It never betrayed or took advantage of you. You felt safe with video games because they couldn't harm you, so you trusted them."

"I felt safe, but I also felt comfortable. Nothing could go wrong in a video game. There's an aspect of strategy and challenge with video games, but the challenge was mostly governed, and the uncertainty could be more easily mitigated compared to real-world scenarios. If I stole a car in *Grand Theft Auto*, I could pause the game, check the map, and find the best escape route. If my castle was destroyed in a computer game, I could reset the game and start over. It wasn't the best way of learning how to adapt to problems and challenges when they happened in reality."

Isabel nodded. "Comfortability led to certainty," she said. "And as we already know, *uncertainty is psychologically unpleasant.* Because you had more control of the outcome, you were more comfortable to indulge in video games."

"Exactly."

"But what would you say about YouTube? You indulged in these videos at a time when you were engulfed in external sources, formulas, frameworks, and secrets on how to live a perfect life— to find fulfillment and happiness."

"The information at the time was too valuable to me. To stop watching was like pulling the plug on an ATM machine that was giving spurting out free money. I trusted YouTube because of the content I watched. It felt like they were giving me all the answers to remedy the pains of my life."

"Yes, Sammy. But both things robbed you of your time. You probably can't recall a single YouTube video you saw last week, nor can you tell me the outcome of the last video game you played. All that time spent is now hyper-localized in a tiny spec in your memory."

She hit on a point I didn't think of before.

YouTube is ubiquitous, unregulated, and free. Drug addictions rob you of your wealth, but YouTube was robbing me of my time. I can always earn dollars, but I will always lose hours (until I learn how to break the fourth dimension, allowing me to perceive time as a physical construct instead of a linear one, but unfortunately, I don't know how to do that just yet).

Video games had an eerily similar effect on me. I don't have detailed memories of the video games I played unless they were put in front of my face. Last month, I was actually digging through my storage space and found the CD of one of the old computer games I played. It rekindled nostalgic parts of my childhood, but I then grounded myself realizing how many hours this thing took away from me: 2,000+ hours of my time were encapsulated in one instance in my memory. I developed some solid hand-eye coordination, but other than that, what a waste of my time.

"*C'est la vie*," say the old folks.

"Ok, I understand now," I told her. "But recognizing that I trust these vices over friends is the tip of the iceberg. I need to fully understand how to trust my friends."

Isabel smiled. "Yes, Sammy. We'll get there soon enough."

She closed her eyes and leaned back into the bench. She seemed to have gone into some form of deep, meditative thought. I still held the chain link in my hand. I looked to see if any aspects of it had changed during our conversation, but I found no visible differences. It was still silver, perfectly intact, and glistening in the moonlight.

My hand started to hover up to my hair before I smacked it away with the other.

"The mural," Isabel said. "It wasn't just the caption; it was the display of friendship that made you stop and look at it for so long."

"Right."

"What about the friends you have now? How would you figure out which ones to trust?"

I paused for a moment to think, but I was struggling to come up with something. Isabel gazed at the palace to admire the Zapotec carvings on the walls, until she threw me a bone to chew on.

"Remember what you told me," she said. "The two personality attributes that you value more than anything else."

"Honesty and humor."

"Right. Who of your friends have these complementary characteristics?"

At that moment, I immediately thought of a specific group of friends. During my senior year of college, I frequently hung out with a core group of about four guys. One day, when one of them (we'll call him Eric) wasn't in the room, the other three started talking about how irritating his drunken shenanigans were getting. They started to bash Eric on how annoying he became when he was drunk and how he'd eventually become a nuisance through the rest of the night.

Their points held validity, but it made me wonder about the things they had said behind my back when I wasn't in the room.

One day, I jokingly asked them. "So, what do you assholes say behind my back when I'm not around?"

Immediately, one of them replied, saying, "Nothing we haven't already said directly to your face."

I immediately felt an off-the-beat epiphanic moment that truly encapsulated how a true friend should act.

I told Isabel that I trust the friends who don't sugarcoat or beat around the bush. They tell me straight to my face— and for my own benefit. People who care about my well-being will stab me in the front instead of the back. They'll tell me when I'm selling myself short. They'll call me an asshole for wasting my talent and skills and settling for something safe or familiar. They'll want me to be successful— even if it meant they wouldn't see or talk to me for long stretches of time.

"I think that's a very noble description," Isabel said. "But what about support? Do you view that trait as valuable as honesty and humor?"

"No, I don't."

Isabel was intrigued, and nodded for me to continue.

"True friends aren't the people who always blindly support you— regardless of how or what you're doing. Inauthentic friends come bundled together with feel-good support statements. These are blanket support statements without any critical analysis or intuitive thoughts on the actual situation."

"I see."

"My honest friends will already be there supporting me if they believed it was something they knew I should be doing, not because it was just objectively good to support your friends. If they're only sitting on my side of the bleachers when the scoreboard is in my favor, then I've made a grave mistake."

"I think that's a great way to put it."

"For the majority of my life, I kept things secret from people to avoid the possibility of it being used as ammunition against me. When I did share something intimate with family or friends (which was rare), I was uncertain about how they would perceive it."

Isabel smiled. "And as we already know, *uncertainty is psychologically unpleasant.*"

"Right. So, for a long time, I just avoided those situations and gave boilerplate answers. I frequently told people I was fine, or that I was happy when I truly wasn't. I didn't share parts of my personal life. It felt comfortable to walk around with this clandestine aura, knowing that no one could use anything against me."

Isabel nodded. "So, what do you understand going forward, Sammy?"

Before I responded, I looked at the chain link curled in my hand, which was still in perfect condition without a crack, fracture, or opening to see. We talked about my friendships, vices, and lack of trust, but still, the chain link remained unchanged.

I looked at it again. It had no opening for other chain links to be attached to it. It was completely sealed off.

This is a pretty useless chain link if it can't be attached to anything else. That's when I realized the real meaning of the chain link.

"I understand I would need to trust my friends and reciprocate that trust and honesty back at them. There are people out there who care about me, and I need to learn how to trust them. I need to bring them into my life and share parts of me that make me vulnerable."

Isabel smiled without teeth from ear to ear. Our silence was interrupted by the sound of a swift clang, as if something metallic was just sliced. I looked down at my hand to see a chunk of the chain link physically cut out.

Now, it had an opening for other chain links to be connected to it. Now, it could be part of a bigger system to hold something together.

Isabel smiled. "In the near future, your feeling of isolation may be a worry of the past."

Chapter 8

I put the broken chain link back in the box and took out the yellow Ticonderoga pencil— the last *artifact* to fix. The lead tip was still broken. Unlike the chain link, this was a clear clue as to what pain it represented; at least, I assumed that was the case.

"What are you thinking, Sammy?" Isabel asked. I held the pencil between my index and thumb and did a flicking motion, so the pencil rotated around the base of my thumb and back into the grip of my index and thumb.

Isabel sat back against the bench, but kept her gaze on me. I was looking at the palace, the intricate geometric patterns on the outer wall, the vast but barren concrete courtyard, the mounds of rock and stone scattered off to the side.

In the distance stood the Church of San Pedro. Its outer walls had the same geometric patterns as the palace with four bright red circular domes on the top, all of them with a cross plunging upwards to the heavens. In the 16th century, the church bustled with devout priests burning incense and performing ritual sacrifices. These people, I thought to myself, followed the rules and guidelines of an ancient book– a book written centuries before their parents and grandparents were born.

Why believe in that idea? Why dedicate your life to live by those ideas?

I took another attentive look at the pencil and thought about myself, the ideas I believed in, and the reasons why I believed them. The pencil started to speak to me in an echo. I couldn't make out the words, but the artifact made more sense, as if it was a representation of my pain– pain in my ideology.

I didn't say a word to Isabel, but she smiled at me without teeth.

———————

December 2, 2018

I could still remember my mother screaming at the top of her lungs, but I chose to tune her out. I was focused on something more important.

I was six or seven years old at the time and I loved to play nature explorer. I would go into the backyard and dig into the small patch of dirt and mud we used to grow plants. I always carried my trusty shovel and bucket to help me. I was quite fond of playing nature explorer, until one day, I dug up a family of worms and quickly transitioned to caretaker. I dug up the worms and put them in my bucket. I would speak to them and ask if they were ok. The winters in Washington were freezing, so I asked if they were warm enough in the dirt. I drew up their replies in my head.

One day, I was playing inside when my mother came downstairs and screamed in terror. I had brought the worms inside and scattered them all over our nice furniture. But while my mother channeled the same decibel as a Navy SEAL drill sergeant, I was calmly talking to my worms.

"It's ok, Mr. Wormy. It's much warmer in here than outside. You'll be safe in here with me."

Isabel rushed downstairs, saw what transpired, and laughed.
My mother, however, was not amused in the slightest.

At that time, I believed that all things were special— even if
they came from dirt.

REALITY

Isabel sat up. "Let's go for another walk."

Isabel led me further through Mitla as we said goodbye to our
view of the palace. I put all the artifacts back in the box, secured the
middle latch, and curled the box in my hand.

The wind was still blowing through the streets, causing the
loose window shutters to clack against the walls of the shops. I looked
up at the stars to see if I could point out the constellations I learned
about when I was 12, but I couldn't.

Slowly, the lines of pastel-colored shops were replaced with
farmland, rows of soil, corn stalk, trees, and bushes. Just like that, Mitla
was far off in the distance and the features of the small *pueblo*
resurfaced.

I couldn't remember the entire walk. Just fragments of it. I felt
as if I was floating in and out of consciousness.

The dirt roads in the *pueblo* remained undisturbed. Not a
sound was heard as we entered. The patrol cars were still gone. The
kids playing in the street were still absent. Nobody was sitting on their

porches. Nobody was driving their cars through the town. Nobody was around.

The dead silence had remained since we left for Mitla. We stopped by a small patch of farmland with rows of corn stalks. Isabel looked down at the dirt and started talking about the worm story.

"I remember your mother got so upset at you that day!" she giggled to herself as we walked further into the *pueblo*. "She will never forget what you did to that couch."

I chuckled. "I didn't know any better. I thought the worms were part of our family."

I couldn't remember the exact story. Isabel had to tell me the story on numerous occasions over the years for it to finally solidify in my head. After the third or fourth time, I slowly started to remember the small details— the color of my shovel, the texture of the dirt, the pattern on the sofa I covered with worms and dirt. Isabel looked up at me and smiled.

"But Sammy, you did know better. You knew something very well that you're struggling with now."

I gave her a perplexed look and she returned a smile as warm as the flame in a furnace.

"The world around you was so beautiful," she beamed. "You took pleasure in seeing the dullest and most mundane parts of the world— *even if they came from the dirt.*"

Isabel bent her knees to get closer to the ground and instructed me to follow suit. I bent down and stared at the soil. She started to dig into the dirt with her hands, until a long, pink cylindrical tube-like body was uncovered. It started to frantically wiggle around in the soil as if it had never seen the sky before. Isabel smiled.

"A worm in dirt will see the world as dirt."

It was an interesting rendition of the Yiddish proverb, but I waited for her to continue.

"There's so much of the world that the worm doesn't see, and so little of what it does. How can this worm see past the life it lives if it's surrounded in the dirt? How will this worm ever see the puffy white clouds in the sky, the vast mountain ranges in the distance, the tall trees surrounding the *pueblo*?"

Isabel pinched the worm with her fingers, lifted it out of the soil as it wiggled around its torso, and placed it in her palm. "The only way is to remove it from the dirt."

She placed the worm in my hands as I watched it wiggle around my palms.

Isabel explained. "The worm you picked up and placed in your home so many years ago was able to see something it previously thought to be non-existent. Even if it's placed back in the soil, it now has a new perspective." Isabel pinched the worm from my hand and placed it back in the dirt.

"I would look at the world— and all parts of it— and laminate it with pure negativity," I said.

Isabel looked content and nodded for me to continue.

"I viewed all aspects of my life with pessimism, because I hated myself as a person and had no one else to blame."

"Yes, Sammy. To address the pains of your ideas, we first need to address the way you look at the world that holds all these ideas.

If you see reality as pessimistic, then all aspects of your reality will become pessimistic."

She was right. Reality will always mirror back my cynical beliefs. I became embroiled under the "means to an end" mentality. That monotony is part of life, and to believe it's full of arching rainbows and valleys of bright red roses is to play ignorant.

Just then, the jingle erupted in my head: *another monotonous day in a monotonous life.*

Nope, not right now.

I would characterize myself as someone who would say that the cause of every divorce is marriage and the cause of every death is life. While objectively, sure, I may be correct, the lens I was looking through was bleak and shrewd. If I was on my deathbed with a terminal disease, my pessimistic outlook on life would nail my coffin shut.

Reality is indifferent when it comes to helping me.

I don't wield some sort of mystical energy that could attract things, nor could I influence aspects of my life by hoping for it. I was unhealthy for a long time, because everything I saw in the world was predicated on pessimism.

"Pessimism is one aspect of your life, Sammy," Isabel added. "But it seeps into all the others. You may view life as suffering, but we can still allow ourselves to live a good life. It makes the suffering just a bit more bearable."

A long silence fell over us. We continued to walk and all I could hear was the crunching and crackling of the dirt. The moonlight illuminated our path forward.

COLLECTIVE IDEOLOGY

— JOURNAL ENTRY 9 —

December 30, 2018

"There's a huge difference between knowing a statistic exists and knowing why it exists."

That was the first thought that entered my head, but before it percolated to the surface, Kristen would continue to verbally erupt like Mt. Vesuvius. She was a college freshman like the rest of us sitting in the class, dead-eyed and hungover at eight o'clock in the morning. It was a core elective class about the social, cultural, and religious institutions of Judaism. I took it to fulfill a requirement so I could transfer to a new college in the fall.

Kristen, however, took it to spew her gospel to a group of binge-drinking freshmen.

The tiny roundtable discussion-style class of 20 wasn't just reserved for the Chosen People, though. Kristen was a devout Christian and every aspect of her life revolved around God. She was raised protestant in North Carolina and regularly attended mass with her equally religious parents. In college, she kept a leather-bound bible and prayed multiple times a day.

I didn't have to do the extra research. She told this to everyone in the class.

I wasn't religious– at least not to Kristen's level. I also wasn't confrontational, so Kristen wasn't blowing up at me. Instead, she aimed her crosshairs at Matthew, who was much more outspoken than I was, sitting on the other side of the large circular table from her.

"You cannot argue with the word of God," she howled at him. "He is the creator of the universe and he loves each and every one of his children. You should love him back!"

Matthew rolled his eyes. He was an outspoken Atheist, but decided to take the class to get a different perspective. He reclined in his chair and took a deep breath.

"How could you love someone who is, by your own words, the creator of all things," he replied. "That includes all things bad, evil, and sinful."

We all sat in awkward silence, looking at each other from across the room. Kristen's face flushed red. "Because he loved us first!" she roared as she rummaged through her backpack to pull out her brown leather-bound bible. "It's in John 4:19. See for yourself."

Kristen extended the bible to Matthew, but he declined.

"I've already read it," he exclaimed, "and it needs a revision."

Kristen was first confused, then angry. Matthew argued that the religious community wasn't as hard-pressed to revise their ancient texts as much as scientists were hard-pressed to rewrite their formulas. There was this air-tight certainty that completely removed doubt, making religion and God these static axioms that never received revisions.

Kristen's face now emanated a bright pink color. She was enraged, completely dismissing what Matthew had said as if she wasn't

listening to him in the first place. He might as well have spoken in
Sanskrit.

She kept reciting passages, trying to bolster her argument.
Matthew looked unamused, slouching in his chair with his arms folded,
until she finally cooled down and scoffed at him.

"I can see you're merely a man without faith."

This piqued Matthew's interest. "I am a man of faith," he
replied while fixing his posture. "But I don't let that faith completely
guide my life."

In that moment, Matthew made me reflect. Faith is different
than reliance on faith. I have no problem with anyone who regularly
attends their local church, temple, or mosque to pray. Faith is a
wonderful social utility for people who have crawled through the
tunnels of Hell and came out the other side— and for others who want
to avoid it altogether. Faith is a great way to maintain a positive
outlook of the future during times of turmoil and for mitigating the
uncertainty of unquestionable and uncontrollable aspects of the world.
The entire class felt a sincere moment of understanding. His statement
fell nicely on everyone, except for Kristen.

"Whatever," she scoffed again. "Religious people live four
years longer than Atheists anyway."

And that's when that first thought crept into my head.

"We're weak as individuals. We have over 800 billion neurons
running through our brains and we still can't properly open clamshell

packaging. Our culture has absolved the need for many of our biological instincts and traits. Firearms reduce the need for physical strength, armies can fight our battles, and farmers can grow our food.

Individually, we're weak, but as a collective, we're strong. Put a lion up against a single person, and the lion will rip him to shreds. But put that same lion up against a community of people, and they'll build a zoo for him and his friends.

We're a social species. We work in tribes, and it's a huge reason why we've flourished. It's crazy how our non-kin tribalism worked, because cooperation among non-kin is almost *non-existent* in the animal world, excluding a few acts of altruism. Our uniqueness among the animal kingdom creates a predisposed condition for us to want to identify with a group. We no longer identify as humans, but rather a subset of humans either by race, religion, or occupation. But collectives sprout ideas, and very much of the time, we believe that people have ideas, when in reality, the ideas have people. While I wish I could pass that line off as my own, Carl Jung beat me to it."

Isabel rolled her eyes. I had started a long rant that made Isabel as unamused by an answer as I've ever seen. This probably wasn't what she expected to hear when she asked me what I thought about the concept of collective ideology. Before, I was telling Isabel about my revelation while I was looking at the Church of San Pedro, but she stopped me halfway through. She said she already knew.

"We already addressed your view of reality," Isabel said.

After putting the worm back in the soil, we walked around the main plaza for quite some time looking for a place to sit, but Isabel passed on every bench or chair or platform we came across. She didn't seem pleased with any of the available seating around the *pueblo,* so we continued to walk.

And walk.

And walk.

After a lot of walking, she asked me about collective ideology, and that's when I gave her a dissertation-length answer that made her head spin.

She verbally ignored me, but gave me a response with her facial expression. We kept walking until we found a place to sit that she looked pleased with (at last)— a bench overlooking a playground made of red metal beams and wooden panels.

There was a tall mast in the middle of the playground with a large sheet draping down from it. The sheet was blue and covered in rips and tears. It rustled as the wind gently blew through it. The silhouette of the mountain range was back in our sight, outlined in the distance.

I rested the box on my lap as we both sat for a moment in silence, looking at the deserted playground. Isabel's hands clasped into each other with an elongated smile stretched over her face. We sat in silence and I started to get anxious. My hand crept its way up to my scalp and started twirling my hair, knotting the strands together, and pulling them out. Isabel let out a faint hum.

"Is that your answer?" she asked.

"It's part of my understanding," I told her while swatting my hand away from my hair. I resisted the urge to grab the pop-up brush from the box.

Isabel hummed. "I see that, Sammy," she said. "But it's not your answer. We want to know why collective ideology is one of your pains."

"Well, it is one of my pains because it insulated my ideas."

Isabel flexed a smile and went back into meditative thought, pressing her back against the bench while humming. After a couple of seconds, she turned to me.

"The *recurrence*," she pointed out. "Do you see it?"

I didn't. Not in the slightest. I thought it would just be wise to throw out a guess. I told her it was my herd mentality, that I was following rules and guidelines that were accepted by the majority.

"No, Sammy," she interjected. "That's an effect of the *recurrence*. I really want you to think. Dig deep into the origination of these collective thoughts."

I thought to myself, but nothing came. "I'm not sure."

Isabel hummed. "When you see an argument, do you automatically try to find ways to disprove it?"

"I would say that it depends on the argument," I said.

Isabel smiled and rested her hand on her lap for a moment.

"If I told you the key to a perfect life was to express as much love and happiness to God as you could, would you believe me?"

"I'm not sure."

"What if I told you that the Moon was made of cheese– would you believe me then?"

"No, absolutely not."

"Why not?"

"Because we've been to the Moon."

"And?"

"It's not made of cheese."

"But you've never been to the Moon, Sammy."

"Yeah, but other people have."

"And do you know these people?"

I gave her a blank look. "No, but I trust them, because they're part of the scientific community, backed by mountains of empirical data and evidence that we can replicate."

"But why do you trust the scientific community?"

"Because formulas, hypotheses, and theories need to be refined over time, and the scientific community is constantly trying to disprove what they already know, searching for a better or clearer answer to understand universal truths."

"So, you trust the scientific community because they proactively go out and try to prove themselves wrong?"

"Exactly. I don't jump off cliffs, because I have faith in the Law of Gravity, and I don't eat expired food because of my understanding of bacteria. Even though I've personally never jumped off a cliff or eaten moldy food, I still believe in what they say. Even though I've personally never been to the Moon, I know it's not made out of cheese."

Isabel smiled but did not reply. The wind blew through the playground, causing a gentle creaking noise from the metal swings.

Isabel sat there in stillness with a smile fixated on her face. I glanced over to my side to make sure I still had the box in my possession sitting by my side. Thank goodness it was. I asked Isabel if she had ever been to this playground, but she ignored my question with a punching statement.

"So, you don't just have faith in science, you also have *reliance*."

"I think that's fair to say," I replied.

I glanced over at the vacant playground, watching the mast flutter with the gentle push of the passing wind. I looked up at the night sky still speckled with the stars in our galaxy, hoping that what I was about to say wouldn't lead to a lightning bolt striking me down from the sky. Isabel smiled.

"What about religion?" she asked. Do you have faith in God?"

"I'm not sure. I can't prove whether God exists or not. We can only somewhat prove that the Gods we've created so far don't exist, but that doesn't mean 'God' exists, because it's also a subjective term."

Isabel nodded for me to continue.

"We use God as a label for what created our universe. That could be anything. It could be a cosmic entity, a superior life form, or a cataclysmic event, like the Big Bang, that led to the creation of our universe. I can't prove whether a God outside of science or the fundamental laws of nature exists or not."

Isabel smiled. "I didn't want to know if you think we can prove God's existence, Sammy. I asked if you *have faith in God*."

At that moment, I thought about Matthew and Kristen . . . and that eventful argument.

"I do believe there is one," I said. "But I won't rely on this belief."

"So, you will put your faith and reliance in science, but not in religion?" Isabel asked.

"Yes, that's right."

"Why?"

I grew up semi-religious in a Reform Jewish household, meaning that the only time we went to temple was for the high holidays, so we could get the cold cuts and deli meat afterward. From high holiday services, my Jewish elementary school, and my Jewish summer camp, I had faith that praying held this omnipotent power that if I just closed my eyes and read the words I memorized from the countless Shabbat ceremonies I attended, then whatever I prayed for would come true. I prayed for so many different things that didn't come true, or didn't materialize in the real world and since. I told Isabel that because of the nature of how religion operates, I can give it my faith, but not my full reliance.

Faith is different from reliance on faith.

"So, the problem," Isabel deduced, "is that too often, *you would substitute faith with reliance.*"

"Right. I would depend on some higher power to cure my problems. Faith with a combination of calculated actions leads to real progress, but faith without action kept me treading water."

Isabel looked pleased. "Yes, Sammy. It's an interesting perspective."

She peered out to the outline of the mountain range in the distance. She hummed to herself and remained in complacency for a moment before focusing her attention on the vacant playground. She calmly said, "But our religious deities aren't the only things we have faith in."

"What do you mean?" I asked.

"We also have faith and reliance on many of the construct humans have developed."

I repeated my initial question to her, as I was still lost. She gleefully smiled and asked me to focus my attention on the playground.

"At night," she said while waving her hand over the playground, "this playground is vacant. But in the morning, it will be covered with infants and toddlers, hanging from the monkey bars and swinging on the swing sets. We have faith that when we let our kids climb, jump, swing, and run around this playground, it won't collapse and hurt any of them."

"Right, but a lot of the time, we can physically see if a playground is sturdy or not. I would never let my kids play on a playground that had monkey bars held together with duct tape and a swing set made of flimsy string and twine."

Isabel smiled. "Yes, that's true," she agreed. "But we also have faith in the fabricated human constructs we can't see."

"Like what?"

"To a degree, we all have faith in the federal reserve, banks, and the stock market. When we invest money into the stock market, we have faith that it will reward us with financial returns over time."

"Right, but we also take calculated actions on how to invest. We do our research in companies that have promising technology, or we play it safe and invest in bonds or broad index funds. What we don't do is throw $10,000 at a random stock and rely on our prayers for it to make us money. If the stock market worked like that, I'd convert my bathroom into a miniature Synagogue."

Isabel chuckled for a moment before returning to a state of calmness. "Your *identity*," she said. "Your *isolation*. The third lock on your box," she added while pointing to it. It was sitting by my side on the bench. "They were all influenced by external sources."

"That's right."

"But it has also seeped into your *ideology*."

My face was painted with shock. "What do you mean?"

"I asked if you would believe me when I said the key to a perfect life is to express as much love and happiness to God."

"Yeah?"

Isabel looked me in the eyes. "Do you believe me, Sammy?"

"I'm not sure. Goals for a perfect life, happiness, and love are subjective to each person. We don't have widely accepted and clearly defined definitions for either of them. I can't disprove your point, because it's a subjective one. Like you said, Tiger Woods can teach me how to play golf, but he can't teach me the true meaning of life."

A gust of wind swept through and rustled the branches of the nearby trees. Isabel smiled.

"You have faith and reliance in science because of how the community operates."

"Right."

"You have faith, but no reliance in religion, because of how the religious community operates."

"Yes."

"You have faith and some reliance in the real and fabricated constructs created by humans, but not without calculated actions."

"I think that's fair to say."

Isabel smiled, emanating an aura of calmness and tranquility. "But you don't have faith or *reliance on yourself*, Sammy. You had faith in external sources, but your faith slowly transformed into reliance. When you talk about external sources, you don't label them as suggestions, reflective stories, metaphors, or motifs. You describe them as rules, guidelines, and principles— all of which are strictly followed. There's little room for interpretation."

This was an ultimate punch to the gut. Isabel opened another door for me to walk through. I let external sources become my religion.

I let them become my God.

I held the pencil between my thumb and index finger, looking intently at its broken lead tip. Isabel seemed to have noticed my intense staring at the pencil.

"Now, do you understand the artifact, Sammy?"

We sat in silence, and in this rare moment, I was the one who smiled. Why the hell did I smile? Isabel just completely dismantled a way of thinking I felt very near and dear to myself. This should be uncomfortable.

But I smiled. It was interesting to hear a new viewpoint. A new perspective. A new way of thinking. I think it's a good indicator of people who have open minds to new ideas.

Remembering that eventful debate in class, I didn't see Kristen smile once. I sighed and held the pencil between the index finger and thumbs of my hands, as if I was reading it like a fortune cookie.

"For so much time," I said, "I let others write my beliefs. I let them put the words down on the page for me, and I simply read the lines like I was an actor in a play. When I was consulting external sources, my pursuit of inner-fulfillment and progression of happiness was molded externally with minimal internal influence. I was given predisposed beliefs about education, career, happiness, trust, friendships, and love that I accepted as fundamental truths. External sources created the collective ideologies that contributed to the insulation of my ideas. New ideas hurt, but they didn't hurt as much as keeping the old ones forever."

I presented the broken tip of the pencil to Isabel. "That's why the lead tip of this pencil is broken. I had been unable to write anything of my own. Nothing holistic, true, authentic, or meaningful."

Isabel flashed a smile without teeth. She seemed satisfied with my understanding.

"Sammy, this is where *scrutiny* comes into play, but before we move forward, do you now see the *recurrence* and the *damage*?"

"I do." I inhaled deeply, letting the cold air fill my lungs, and decompressed my chest. "My *reliance* was on the external sources that created the collective ideologies that I blindly followed. Once I grasped onto an idea I believed, I would insulate myself with articles, books, lectures, blogs, and a truckload of other forms of content to support my belief. Instead of constructing the world around me, I let them do it for me with little pushback or *scrutiny*. I lost a huge chunk of my critical thinking and skepticism. This was the *damage*."

This time I was satisfied with myself. It finally felt like I was able to dislodge one of the rocks stuck in my cave to let the light shine through. It was a crucial step to take.

I smiled, and so did Isabel. I realized that I should smile more often. It takes less muscles, anyway.

———————

I looked up at the moonlight and then back at the pencil. The lead tip was still broken. I furrowed my brow at it, like I was expecting some sort of explanation as to why it hadn't changed.

I should try and channel my magical powers of restoration.

"It's not as easy as the other *artifacts*," Isabel said with a chuckle. She was looking up at the moonlight, letting the glow shine into her eyes. "We need to build scrutiny," she added. She sat in silence for a moment, letting the bright glow of the moon overtake her eyes. I kept fiddling with the broken pencil in my hands, growing impatient.

"So how do I build scrutiny?" I asked.

Isabel smiled and turned to me, gazing at me with her dark marble eyes. "Scrutiny only comes when you have consciously decided to evaluate a certain statement. Your ideas need to have malleability—to have the thought in the back of your head that you may be wrong about what you currently believe in."

"Okay."

"I'd love for you to play along in a quick thought experiment."

I nodded and she smiled.

"TSA has never stopped a terrorist attack," she declared. "Abraham Lincoln was opposed to racial equality, and Mother Theresa ran a hospice center in Calcutta that lacked proper medical care."

We sat in silence for a moment. Isabel asked, "Now, what's your first thought about these statements?"

"They're jarring."

"How so?"

"Well, they go against the grain of how we view certain people and organizations."

"Right."

"But why did you bring them up?"

Isabel smiled. "Well to make things clear, I don't bring these up to force you to believe the opposite. I'm not telling you to believe that the TSA is useless. I'm not telling you to believe that Mother Theresa was driven by the suffering and death of others. I'm not telling you to believe that Abraham Lincoln was a full-blown racist."

"Then what are you saying?"

"What I am saying is that you need this information to make complete and rational judgments."

"I see."

"Why do you believe the TSA is safe? Maybe because it's supported by the federal government, or because you feel safe every time you put your 3-ounce bottle of shampoo in the X-ray and walk through a metal detector. What about Mother Theresa? Why do you think she has a heart of gold? Maybe it's because of all the statues that were erected after her death, or because of all the charity organizations she built to help people dying of diseases, like leprosy and tuberculosis."

It was an interesting point. I probably have views in my head that are so concrete, it would blunt a rock axe to a nub.

Isabel continued, "The same things can be said about Lincoln, Gandhi, the Federal Reserve, socialism."

"And about fulfillment, happiness, pain, and suffering," I added.

"Exactly. You need to increase your peripheral vision of the world. You need to constantly reflect and challenge what you think you already know. Use first principle thinking if you have to, digging down to the nucleus of your thoughts to find the fundamental truths. Ask yourself a series of questions. *Why do I believe what I believe? When did I start believing this? What if I believed in the opposite?*"

I could see the picture that Isabel was painting. I would need to consume the facts, whether they supported or dismantled my current view. With external sources, I believed things that made me feel better as a person or gave me a fabricated sense of the world, instead of looking at things in a more rational and objective way. Isabel looked satisfied.

"We have subconscious thinking," she added. "And subconscious answers for certain things based on the groups we're a part of. This isn't to say that collective ideology is bad or necessarily evil. It's actually fundamental. But acknowledging that your views may be greatly influenced by a collective helps you become more critical and skeptical."

I smiled with interest and Isabel looked quite content with my understanding, but I nudged her again.

"Okay that all sounds nice and everything, but again, how do I build scrutiny?"

Isabel smiled and looked back up at the star-speckled sky.

"Your sips are turning into gulps. It's best to slow down to make sure you don't choke."

Isabel smiled. "Let's start with how ideas are presented and absorbed." I sat back and nodded, pretending like I knew where she was going.

"When you're presented with a statement," she premised. "What's the first thought that comes to mind?"

"I mean, it depends on the statement."

"What was the first thought that came to mind when I said the TSA has never stopped a terrorist attack?"

"I thought, 'Woah, I had no idea,' because it was something that never occurred to me."

"And then what happened?"

"Well, I believed it."

I realized at that moment that I applied the same type of rational thinking to when I was consulting external sources. Their ideas were novel and unique, so I didn't have a proper screening process for believing or scrutinizing them. Most of the ideas that weren't totally out of left field were automatically accepted as fact. I felt Isabel transmitting an image into my head.

"We need to understand the flow of beliefs in order to create scrutiny," Isabel said. "Anytime we're presented with a statement, our brain always takes one of three paths: acceptance, rejection, or scrutiny. These lead to either acceptance or rejection."

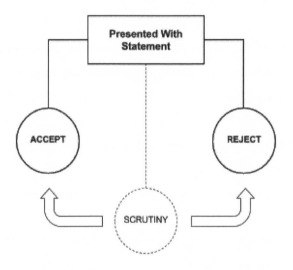

"To some degree," Isabel continued, "we always need to make sure we go down the path of scrutiny first, so we can come to an educated conclusion. We keep our thoughts malleable and avoid neurological laziness by blindly accepting and rejecting statements without some form of vetting."

I saw this many times while I was engulfed in external sources, where the content of certain figures was automatically accepted without scrutiny. Like Kristen, whose thought process auto-defaulted to rejection when it came to listening to points made by Matthew, mine went to acceptance when it was spoken by external sources.

"What's a good way to develop scrutiny in your life, Sammy?" Isabel asked.

"I would say empirical knowledge or evidence."

"That's a good start. You also said there's this air-tight certainty that completely removed doubt when it came to God and religion."

"Yes, we have faith but also sometimes *reliance on faith*, creating less than desirable outcomes. Instead of learning about the mechanisms that make the world operate, we can attribute the answer as a design by God. Instead of seeking established and proven treatment, we can rely on our prayers so that God will expunge the sickness from our bodies."

Isabel smiled. "So how do God and religion relate to scrutiny?"

"It relates to scrutiny because they're axioms. If I rely on them to provide me with answers, I won't have the urge or inkling to seek a better answer myself."

"Exactly."

"I'll try to use a form of empirical knowledge to come to conclusions about myself and the world around me. When I experience life events, I'll strongly hesitate to attribute them to a static axiom or doctrine, so I can avoid becoming just a tad myopic in my views."

"But you can't be rational about everything in the world," Isabel noted.

"I know that, and I concede that's true."

Isabel smiled and nodded for me to continue.

"I don't speak about what I know, but rather I inquire about what I *don't* know. And when I do inquire, I use a foundational layer of something I wish I had adopted a long time ago— scrutiny."

Isabel smiled. Despite my large gulps, I didn't drown.

RELATIONSHIPS

— JOURNAL ENTRY 8 —

December 23, 2018

I already know this story and I don't need to write a journal entry for me to reflect on it. Love is the most painful and most powerful thing I have ever experienced.

———————

I gripped the pencil in my hand, tip up, like I was carrying a torch. It remained unchanged. The lead tip was still broken. Isabel stood up and pressed her hands into her lower back.

"We've been sitting for too long," she said. "Let's go for another walk."

I put the pencil back in the box and secured the middle latch. Isabel led us on a dirt path back into the *pueblo*. The crunching and crackling of the dirt filled the air. We took a few turns and ended up walking uphill on a dirt road lined with the brick walls of houses.

Some of them had old wooden shutters, but they were all closed. One wall was made of concrete and painted in bright but faded blue. The roads were dilapidated. Rubble from rocks were paved over to the sides to clear the road. The walls were high, but not high enough where we couldn't see the mountain range in between the gaps of houses.

Isabel walked patiently with her hands behind her back. I had the box locked and curled in my right hand.

"Why didn't you ever remarry?" I asked Isabel curiously.

She hummed and ignored my question, just as she ignored all of my personal questions about her. I was mildly irked. The crunching and crackling of the dirt became louder.

"I think that was a fair question," I added.

"Fair? Yes," she said. "But not a relevant one." She continued to hum to herself, walking patiently with her hands folded behind her back.

"Why isn't it relevant?" I asked.

She smiled. "We're here to talk about you, and you didn't just ask that question out of curiosity."

I was about to say something, but I inaudibly stammered. The words couldn't leave my mouth. It felt like my jaw could not unhinge itself. Isabel shot me a kind smirk.

"Sammy, why don't you tell me about your relationships."

"Why should I do that?"

Isabel gave me a kind smile. "Because it will be a more fruitful conversation to learn about your relationships than to know about my marital choices."

I almost guffawed when she said "relationships." I was awful at relationships in general. Monogamy has gotten harder, even harder than getting a Friday night reservation at Dorsia.

I laughed in my head. Isabel remained stone-faced. I mustered the gumption to get the words out of my mouth.

"Well, I'm awful at relationships, but not by choice."

Isabel narrowed her eyes. "Why do you say that?"

"Because I hate the idea of marriage."

Isabel raised an eyebrow in speculative interest.

"In my mind, *marriage sucks* and it's become an industry-standard instead of a choice. I think it acts as a front for people to conceal their actual problems. It feels like putting on social-induced shackles to seem loyal and committed. I don't see marriage as a new sentence at the beginning of a new chapter, but instead, I see it as a death sentence. But then again, this was just a vapid excuse . . . one I probably didn't even believe," I said.

Isabel deflated even more, as if someone bear-hugged all the air out of her. "You're avoiding the question by giving an answer you don't truly believe. This is something difficult for you to share, something very intimate."

How the hell does she know all my thoughts? I stuttered in my speech, unable to form a complete sentence. Isabel smiled.

"Sammy, if we wanted to critique the marriage industry, then your answer may have some merit, but it's not your answer. I don't want the answer from science. I don't want the answer from marriage. I want the answer from *you*. What do you believe? What do you value?"

I flexed my brow. My beliefs about relationships always seemed to come from an objective school of thought, but they were coupled with little to none of my own beliefs.

"I'm not sure how to answer that," I told her.

Isabel smiled. "That's ok. How about we find the answer? Tell me how you would treat your partner?"

"I guess . . ." the words slowly trickled out of my mouth before Isabel interrupted me.

"Sammy, I know you may not be sure about these answers, but remember the importance of conviction."

A gust of wind blew through the branches of the nearby trees. I took in a deep breath and exhaled.

"Okay . . . well, first, I wouldn't call myself a knight in chivalrous armor, but I do my best to treat my partner as equal."

"And how do you do that?"

"I don't put her on a pedestal, and I don't try to make the relationship revolve entirely around her."

"Have you done this in the past?"

"All the time, because I would jump into relationships and quickly become codependent. I was inadvertently using them as support systems. I needed them more than they needed me, so I gave them so much more than was necessary."

Isabel nodded. "And have you had a relationship that felt pure? That felt equal? That felt like both pedestals were at the same height?"

I thought to myself as I sifted through the imaginary Rolodex of breakups in my head. Most of them were amicable, but nonetheless difficult. We kept walking through the walls of brick and concrete until a small patch of dead grass, no bigger than the size of a basketball court, was put between two of the walls on the left side of the street. It was placed between two of the brick houses, as if it was perfectly cut out from a video game.

Like the small homes it nestled between, the patch of grass was uphill, and in the middle there was a small and shriveled cherry blossom tree (I would later find out it was a staghorn sumac). Small brown bushes were scattered around the patch of grass, some of them displaying a few green leaves, but the pink leaves of the cherry blossom popped out.

The wind blew and the branches quivered, releasing some of the leaves and letting them fall to the ground. There was nothing behind the tree to take away your attention from it, nor was there anything in front blocking it from your view. It was decadent.

I thought of an old tree that stood for many years at a summer camp I went to. It was a different camp, one that didn't let me eat double-decker PB&Js at 10 o'clock at night. And that thought of a tree rekindled a memory of a past relationship.

"I did have a relationship once, at summer camp," I told Isabel. She had left me in silence for the last few moments, so my answer caught her attention as she immediately turned her head to me.

"Tell me about it, Sammy."

I hesitated. "But I was so young. I don't know if I would count it as a real relationship."

"You may be right," she said with a smile. "But we might be able to find something valuable."

I became more hesitant. This was young, stupid, and giddy love, where 98% of our time spent together was amazing, while the other 2% of the time was spent fighting about a text that one of us misinterpreted. But maybe it was healthy to revisit this experience. A gentle wind blew through the cherry blossom. More leaves fell down.

I orated. "Well, we were both camp counselors. I was 19 or 20 at the time, and she was a year younger. We knew each other through mutual friends, but we never had a long-form conversation with each other."

Isabel interrupted me. "Tell me about her, Sammy. What did she look like?"

I closed my eyes and thought about her appearance. The long and vibrant black hair that went down to her chest. The dark and thick eyebrows with tails tales that curved down toward her temples. The brown freckles spattered over her cheeks and the brim of her nose.

I thought intensely. It had been years since I'd seen her, so some of the details were missing. There were parts about *her* I was missing.

I opened my eyes. Her vibrant black hair rustled as a gust of wind blew by. She rested one hand on the trunk of the cherry blossom, wearing the outfit I always saw her wear— a black and white striped T-shirt, blue jeans, and Converse sneakers. She looked intently at me, and I gave the same look back. Isabel smiled.

"How did you two meet?"

I didn't know if she could see her. We were both looking in the same direction, but she was unmoved. She kept staring at me, and I didn't break my gaze. I continued to talk to Isabel.

"A couple of days before the campers would arrive, all the counselors walked a few miles to a nearby campsite in the woods. The 20 of us gathered around a roaring campfire and talked amongst each other. Then I saw her."

She gave a modest smile and slowly walked down the hill.

"What happened next?" Isabel asked. I had paused the story to look at her. A loss of words in the moment. I tried to concentrate.

"It's weird, I— I don't remember a single thing we talked about," I said. "Maybe because I was so distracted by her. The sharp contrast of the night and the hot yellow and orange glow of the fire made her skin shine and her eyes glisten."

She kept walking downhill until she was at arm's length from me. She bit her lip and ran her hand through her long thick black hair. Her bright hazel eyes lit up like yellow fireworks. I swallowed hard.

"We talked for what felt like hours, but it was probably much shorter than that."

She raised an eyebrow at me. Apparently, it was for hours.

"A few nights later, our two cabins went stargazing and we had our first kiss under an old tree."

I couldn't remember the name of the tree. If I heard it once, I would know immediately. She giggled at me like she knew the answer, but enjoyed watching me struggle to remember. I mouthed *SHUT UP* to her. She kept giggling.

"And then what happened?" Isabel asked.

"After that, we saw each other every day. Our cabin of campers would cross paths all the time, but we would spend most of our free nights together. We would sit in a hammock together for hours, talking about anything. We talked about some of our incompetent campers, we talked about each other, we talked about our futures, we talked about nonsense. When I was with her, I felt different."

She smiled and Isabel hummed as she continued to watch the petals fall from the cherry blossom. "What made this relationship stand out to you the most?" she asked.

I looked at her for an answer and she gave me a look back. It was a look that said, *"I'm waiting for you to say something really sweet about me."*

I exhaled.

"Many things. Many things visually, symbolically, and ritualistically. Every morning after breakfast, we had morning prayers, which I absolutely hated. But she was there."

She flexed her cheeks, puffing out her freckles– the little brown specks that I always found cute.

I turned my head to Isabel "You see," I said while pointing to my cheek. "I have these three birthmarks on my cheek, all relatively equidistant from each other. She would always call them the Bermuda Triangle."

Isabel continued to focus on the tree, but *She* took a step closer to me and rested her hand on my cheek. I turned my head to look at her penetrating eyes. Those beautiful hazel eyes. Her touch was warm. My lips curved.

"But I don't think I'll ever have the same feeling of what I experienced," I deflated. "To be in a community with people you love, disconnected from the outside world, and every day, during these mandatory morning prayers, you can look over to the other side of the amphitheater and make eye contact with a woman who could move you with her eyes while hearing the hymns of 100 people in unison."

She rubbed my cheek and I smiled bigger. "Like an uncut gem," I said, while looking into her eyes. "This love was pure and unrefined."

I looked back at Isabel. She hummed, but then fixed her attention back at me. She shot me one of the kindest smiles I'd seen so far. I was finally putting some heart into these answers and I felt like she was proud of me for that.

"What happened after camp ended?" she asked.

I looked back at *Her*. Her smile inverted. Her dimples went soft and the glow from her presence had briefly faded. Her hand left my cheek.

"We had to rub our eyes to get out all the happy-go-lucky utopian charms that were stuck in there and lug ourselves back to the real world."

"Did you live close to each other?"

"No. We went to different schools across the country. We tried to maintain the relationship, but it didn't work out."

"How did you take the breakup?"

"I think pretty well."

She narrowed her thick dark eyebrows at me. "Ok, maybe I acted bitter and immature for a bit of time," I corrected myself.

She gave me a satisfied look and rubbed my cheek again.

"But she could have been your future partner," Isabel said. "Do you think that could have been a possibility?"

I looked at *Her*. She gave a faint smile. A smile that tried to remain positive while addressing the uncertainty. "Absolutely, and I still believe that to this day. But not at that time. It would have caused more damage than good."

"How would it have been more damaging?"

"We both got more involved and invested in the relationship, and there was a bit of thought about whether either one of us would move so that we could be closer to each other."

"And why didn't either of you move for each other?"

"I thought it was foolish. She was attending a college with a phenomenal pedigree, as was I. I didn't want to take that from her, and I don't think she wanted to, either."

Then again, I wasn't sure if she thought that. *She* narrowed her dark and thick eyebrows at me again. I felt this time it was for something less trivial. Maybe I was wrong, maybe this was just my perception of the relationship, maybe I never told her any of this, or maybe I just thought about it.

She could have seen it in a completely different way. I looked over at Isabel, who dimpled her cheeks.

"Do you now see what you value?" she asked.

I tapped my fist against my lips. I decided to dig my heels and think deeper into the relationship. I looked back at *Her*, directly into her glistening hazel eyes. A gust of wind blew through her hair and briefly covered her face.

"I guess I can say what I thought at the time." I took her hands in mine. They were warm, so I felt like I was wearing a pair of wool mittens.

"I really cared about this woman, and I knew if she moved closer to me, she would be temporarily happier . . . but the decision would have long-term consequences. She was attending a prestigious university and pursuing a lucrative science career— I didn't want to take any of that away from her and stifle her ambitions."

"And why did you do that?" Isabel asked. "You had to let go of something you really cared about."

She smiled and I squeezed her hand harder. "I did. But most of my past relationships made me think about what was best for me. Maybe because I didn't want to hurt her, because I cared about her so much."

"Usually, when we care about someone, we keep them as close to us as we can. But why did you let her go?"

I exhaled and let go of her hand. "Because *I'd rather see a friend flourish than a partner suffer.* This wasn't about me or what I wanted . . . it was about what was best for *both* of us."

A gentle wind bustled through the branches of the cherry blossom. Bright pink leaves were scattered across the dead brown grass. A bright glow faded, and Isabel was looking intently at the tree, as was I. There were no footsteps in the dirt. We sat in a long silence.

"Did you love her?" she asked.

"I did, but she already knew that. Love is such a vague and nebulous word, but if I had to give it a finite definition, I would say that love is when you care about something more than you care about yourself. Robin Williams said this about true loss in *Good Will Hunting,* but I also equate it to true gain. I won't experience true loss until I lose something I cared more about than myself, and I won't experience true love until I find something I care about more than I care about myself. So, with that definition, yes I loved her."

"But at the time, you didn't love yourself?"

"Yeah." My tone started to deflate. "I was dealing with many of the same pains we've already talked about."

"Do you think that could have played a role in the relationship?

"I hear a lot of people say that they can't organically love someone until they can love themselves, but I think that's a romantic fallacy."

Isabel raised a kind eyebrow. "And why's that?"

I exhaled. "I believed the idiom for a long time, but there wasn't an objective way to tell whether I loved myself or not. But if I opened myself up to be loved by someone, I could, in turn, learn to love myself in a similar way. I didn't understand this concept at the time, but it was something I intuitively knew.

Isabel hummed. "You said you'd rather see a *friend flourish than a partner suffer.*"

"Yes."

"But you wanted to keep her in your life?"

"Yes, I did."

"Why did you want to do that? Was it painful to have reminders of her and to not be with her?"

"Yes, it was painful, as it's painful for anyone else who has gone through a breakup. But it wasn't the most painful part."

"What do you mean?"

"In my experience, the worst part of the relationship isn't the fighting, the awkward silences, or even the breakup. I don't think it's any of those. *It's when you forget about that person as they slowly become less of a part of your life.* The worst part is when you forget about how much you cared about that person, when you forget about what you would do for that person. The breakup isn't the worst, because all of those thoughts are intensified. It's when you truly think about all of those things the most. But after a couple of weeks or months, you'll stop having those thoughts, and your partner will just be another name in your phone that you don't call anymore."

"I see."

"I didn't want her to become that person in my life. So, if I could have her in any aspect in my life— having her as a friend would be less painful than having her completely vacant."

Isabel smiled. "Do you still not count this relationship?"

"No, I do count it. In fact, it may be one of the most important ones I've ever had."

"Yes, Sammy I think so, too. So, do you have a better understanding now of what you value and believe in relationships?"

"I do, Isabel. I do."

We both took one last look at the cherry blossom before walking further down the dirt road. I had more to write in my journal than I thought.

HAPPINESS

One of the most vivid memories I have as a child was when my father took me to watch airplanes take off and land at the Santa Monica Airport when I was about 10 years old. For three hours, I stood outside, leaning forward on a chain-link fence in complete awe from watching the planes take off and land. I thought about that distinct memory for a long time and why it remained so vivid inside my head ever since then.

Was it because growing up, I didn't spend a lot of alone time with my father, and this moment was very important?

I don't think so. I don't even remember anything specific he said to me that day. There weren't any valuable life lessons or moments transmitted in our conversation. I only remember that he drove me in his blue 1991 Honda Civic.

Was it because something happened that day?

Nope. Nothing specifically novel happened. I didn't see a Gulfstream hit some turbulence on its way down and obliterate to pieces on the tarmac, nor did I see a Chicago Red Sox fan streaking on the airstrip.

Was it because I loved planes?

Maybe, but it's not the reason. I liked planes as they frequently made appearances during playtime, along with my army soldiers and Hotwheels cars— but I didn't love them. They were just another kind of toy I liked to play with.

This memory sticks out the most, not because I was with my father or because I liked planes, but because of the actual function of planes. The function of taking off and landing. To depart from one place and arrive in another. It symbolizes the embryo and completed stages of a person's metamorphic journey: to start as one person and end as another.

But on that day, I remember seeing something I never saw a plane do: approach the airport ready to land, with its landing gear folded up and wings retracted, when, at the last minute, it flies over the runway. I later learned that this was called a "balked" landing, but at the time, when I asked my father why the plane did that, I remember him saying something along the lines of, "The plane just wasn't ready to land."

I always saw planes in two (and only two) states: taking off and landing. But there's an enormous gap between the two states that account for the other 99% of the journey, such as the plane flying in the air, heading toward its destination. There's so much more to taking off and landing, but I just don't really understand it yet.

For a moment, I gazed over at the silhouette of the mountain range in the distance. A feeling rushed into my head. I looked over the landscape of the *pueblo* and realized something I hadn't realized in a long time. My presence was undisturbed, and I had felt as if this moment was one without any additional need or desire. That's when I realized that I could understand happiness.

"Isabel—" I said. "I think I can understand this one myself."

She shifted her attention to me and smiled. "Ok, Sammy," she said with a nod. I took a deep breath.

"Thinking about happiness and unhappiness, these two options I've had all my life . . . two restricted options that gave no room to wiggle or squirm.

But now, I don't see happiness as binary— whether I'm either happy or unhappy. I see happiness as incremental steps of upward progress. There's no cheat code in life that will help me quantum leap toward pure happiness. Too often, I imagined that achieving my goals would make me happy, when in actuality, it's making *progress* towards them that made me a happier person. I'm less focused on the takeoff and the landing, and more focused on time spent in the air.

I also think the pursuit of a permanent state of happiness will evolve into an unquenchable desire that will erode my core if I continue to participate. It's what I tried to do while I was consulting external sources, and I came out even more miserable than I was before. Happiness isn't a state— it's continual progression forward, and I need to define that continual progression forward for myself. Nobody else can define what happiness is for me, nor can they define my love or fulfillment. So, I must do it myself.

I want to predicate my happiness on not feeling an urge to fill any physical or emotional needs. I want to be as close to total satisfaction as I can be. I now understand the meaning of the Mandarin duck. We perceive them as happy, because they appear to be *absent* from any pain or suffering. They're proper, put together, and *absent* of any lifestyle blemishes and boils. My happiness runs parallel with *absence* and understanding that if there isn't anything else I need, I can be content with what I have and who I am.

As I'm speaking right now, if I had to gauge it— I would say that I'm not very happy with myself overall. Yes, there are days when I'm happy and other days when I'm not, but I know for a fact that I'm way happier than when I was in middle school, high school, college, during my first job, last year, last month, last week, and even yesterday. I'm getting closer, and that's my true meaning of happiness."

Isabel nodded at me, flashed a large smile, and put her hand on my knee. "I think we've talked about all that's needed to be said."

She was satisfied, but I wasn't— at least, not yet.

ENLIGHTENMENT

I felt deflated. There was one last pain on my list that I wanted to understand, but Isabel declined to talk further. We walked through the *pueblo* on a dirt path back to the house. The trees were still rustling from the wind and the silence remained in the air.

As we approached the door, a new question erupted in my head— one that I couldn't go without asking.

"I'm not satisfied," I proclaimed. She was walking ahead of me, so she turned around abruptly and inflated her dimples.

"And why is that, Sammy?"

I swallowed hard. "How will I know?"

We both stood still. The crunching and crackling of the dirt had stopped. Isabel flexed her brow.

"How will you know what?" she asked.

"How will I know when I truly understand myself? How will I know when these words can be set into stone? How will I know when all that I have believed and instilled in my life has worked? How will I know when I'm enlightened?"

My erraticism turned one question into four, but they all shared the same point. She hummed and flexed a meditative smile. She looked up at the sky to see the bright crescent moon slowly descend into the peaks of the mountain range.

"The night is fading away."

She sat on one of the steps in front of the entrance to the house and gestured for me to sit beside her. I sat between her and a beautiful part of her garden, sprawling with leaves, flowers, and fruits, painted with a bright white glow from the moonlight. Isabel hummed again.

"Why would you look for something you don't know how to find?"

"What do you mean?"

"Why would you look for something when you don't know what it looks like? Why would you look for something that has no appearance? No shape or color. No hardness or softness. No height or width. No weight or buoyancy. Why would you search for something like this?"

I shook my head at her answer. It didn't make sense.

"But we've been doing that this whole time!" I exclaimed. "We've been searching for things like enlightenment. What about my *identity*, my *isolation*, my *ideology*? None of these have an appearance. They don't have any of the attributes you just described."

"Yes, but we aren't searching for them. They are merely containers, just as *Enlightenment* is a container in its own right. You need to fill it with something."

"Fill it with what?"

Isabel flashed a smile while hiding her teeth. "Do you know what we have been doing this whole time?"

I flexed my brow at her. She chuckled and looked up at the stars. She let out a meditative hum and smiled back at me.

"Sammy, we've been filling your containers."

I was about to speak, but shut my mouth before I could. My hand was about to reach for my hair, but I used the other to hold it down. I remained silent, but the lightbulb in my head started to flicker.

Isabel smiled and gently rested her hand on my knee.

"We filled your *Identity* container with your passion pursuits, the ones that caused you so much turmoil. We filled it with your positive and fabricated personality, but also with your honest and humorous one. We filled it with your ADHD, anxiety, and depression, but also with your new definition of your mental health.

We filled your *Isolation* container with your friendships– the inauthentic ones, but also the authentic ones. We filled it with your vices, but also your trust in those vices. We filled it with your blind altruism, but also your new rule of treating others.

We filled your *Ideology* container with your pessimism, but also your newfound optimism. We filled it with your dependence on collective ideology, but also your new view of scrutiny. We filled it with your relationship with your first love, your first true heartbreak, but also with your definition of love. We filled it with your *absence* of the desire to need more in life, that you described as *Happiness*— another empty container until it is filled with something that is meaningful to you."

She lifted her hand off my knee and looked me in the eyes. It was the first time I noticed her soft brown eyes, staring at me with such love and reverence.

"Do you now know when you will be enlightened, Sammy?"

I looked around her circular lawn and then built a mental image of the *pueblo* in my head. Isabel had built her own form of enlightenment.

"I shouldn't seek enlightenment because enlightenment has no container. Setting enlightenment as my goal is like setting the sky as my target if I was an archer— I'll never know when I hit it. I haven't reached enlightenment yet. I haven't found my answer, nor have I solved all my pain and suffering. Some questions don't have an answer, and some pains don't have a cure. I'll never be completely fulfilled, nor will I ever be completely happy. I'll always be a work in progress, and I may never be fully complete until I'm lying in my casket. Enlightenment has no relevance to my life, because my life will never have a climax, or an end, or a finish. I will always learn, I will always change, and I will always progress."

Isabel radiated a soft smile. A brief silence carried over us. Then, a faint whirring and humming noise came from inside the box. I unlocked the middle latch and lifted the lid. I pulled out the pencil to see the lead tip sharpened to a needle's point.

I could finally become the author of my own beliefs.

Isabel gave me a pleased look and gazed up at the stars. They started to fade as the faint glow of the sun crept up from behind the horizon.

"We are losing the night," she said. "There's one last thing we should do."

— *JOURNAL ENTRY 21* —

March 24, 2019

This entry is a bit of a cop out. But it's also not my fault, because I don't remember any of it happening. And I was six years old (curse you, infantile amnesia).

Isabel had to tell me the story. Multiple times. And each time, it warms my heart.

I felt like I was a fairly easy kid to parent. I was a rule-follower. I rarely snuck out, yelled at my parents, or disobeyed strict directions. I was also quiet and reserved. I didn't talk to anyone. Adam was the loud and bombastic one. The one with what Isabel would call the 'big boca' (boca is mouth in Spanish).

What was even more interesting about me was that it was hard to punish me when I did break the rules or did something wrong. In the beginning, Isabel would try to take away something I liked in order to get me to finish my homework or eat my veggies.

"If you don't eat these veggies, we won't watch Lion King no more!" she would say to me.

*"Oh, it's ok," I would tell her. "I've already seen it before.
You can take it away."*

*This would puzzle Isabel, as well as my parents. But mostly
Isabel, because she had to figure out a way to give me some carrot stick
motivation, or to find some leverage.*

*"Sammy," she'd say. "If you finish these veggies on your
plate, we can watch Dragon Tales."*

*She waved the VHS cover of the colorful cartoon dragons
flying in the air with the two main characters (a brother and sister)
riding on their backs. I gently shook my head.*

*"It's okay, Isabel," I would calmly tell her. "I've already seen
that episode."*

*She tried everything: dangling or restricting my favorite toys
("Oh, that's okay. I've already played with those action figures"),
cartoons I hadn't seen ("Oh, that's okay. I'll just watch a different
show"), and my favorite foods ("Oh, that's okay. I'll just eat something
else").*

*But she finally broke through to me. And I can't believe as I'm
writing this journal entry that I forgot what I did . . . what I did to make
Isabel act this way. But I did something, and she wasn't happy. She was
more than unhappy, she was disappointed. And that tore through me
deeper than the loss of any cartoon dragon or any favorite action
figure could. And I listened.*

*Because if I didn't listen to Isabel, I would disappoint her. She
had given me so much in my life, so the last thing I ever wanted to do
was to make her feel that way. And I made sure she never did.*

I was disappointed. I had one last pain in mind to discuss, but Isabel seemed fixated in a different direction. She focused her attention onto the box that sat by my side. She instructed me to pick it up and place it on my lap. I opened the box to see the baby blue pop-up brush and the silver chain link. I put the sharp-tipped pencil inside with them. Under all the artifacts was the same severed head of the green rose in perfect condition.

Isabel walked over to her shed and returned with a metal hammer. She told me to take the hammer and smash the box. I refused.

She nudged me. "It's okay, Sammy, I insist."

I got agitated and my voice grew in volume.

"No!" I said as I stood my ground. "Why do you want me to break the box we spent so much time opening?"

Isabel smiled. "The box has been opened. There's no need for it anymore."

"But I do need it. It's the place where I can hold my artifacts."

Isabel shook her head. "Sammy, keeping the box around is more harmful than destroying it."

My voice launched up in octaves. I became furious. I started trembling as my emotions took over my speech. I started to cross-examine Isabel as if she was guilty of a capital crime.

"Why is it more harmful? I want to know!" I shouted.

Isabel remained calm, fixing a wide smile on her face. I stood up, flailing my arms in the air.

"Why won't you tell me? Why do I have to do this?"

I was sobbing. Tears rolled down my cheeks. I started walking in circles, trying to reserve my emotions (but without luck). I opened the box to look at the artifacts again. A tear dropped from the corner of my eye into the box. It dripped onto the pop-up hairbrush and over its circle surface.

Isabel broke her silence.

"You need to open yourself up to the world," she instructed. "The box is preventing you from doing that. It's the last thing you must do."

I closed the box and clutched it to my chest.

My sobbing intensified. "What do you mean? What are you talking about? We opened the box so that I could understand my pains. The box is open now, why do I need to destroy it?"

"Because as long as the box exists, it can be closed, it can be locked, and it can be stored away forever."

I made eye contact with Isabel. The tears continued to well into my eyelids. Isabel picked up the hammer.

"Only you can do this, Sammy. Not me or anyone else."

I knelt down to the ground, my face inches away from the dirt as I clutched the box to my chest. Isabel sat in silence.

"How do I know that breaking this box will help me?"

"You don't know. It's uncertain. And *uncertainty is psychologically unpleasant.*"

The tears stopped coming. I got my breathing under control. I froze my body and thoughts in place. Then, a new thought percolated in my head. A new aspect of my life. One that felt unteachable: *Responsibility.*

Isabel wasn't asking me to break the box to relieve me of all my pains; she was asking me to break the vessel that kept them around. The container that kept them around long enough to seep, burrow, and infiltrate into all aspects of my life.

Pain will inevitably return in my life. It will come in shapes and forms I had never seen before. But I will do everything in my power to face them. I will use all my power to not blame anyone or anything for when they come back— no matter how large or lingering they become.

I will use all my power to not let parts about me I can't change serve as excuses for the pain. I cannot control how often or how tortuous the pain will be, only how I perceive it. I will use all my power to understand that I can experience pain, despite who I am, that the pain I experience can be serious, and that I have the ability to understand and remedy it. The pain will come back and when it does, I will face it with a decorated coat of *Responsibility*.

I gathered myself. I wiped the leftover tears from my cheeks and blew my nose into my shirt. I stood up again and looked at Isabel sitting on the front step to the house. I looked into the main room of her house through the giant window. It was still barren, the same way we left it. Isabel smiled and placed the hammer at her side, waiting for me to pick it up.

"Take the artifacts out," she said. "You should keep them."

The straps were never locked, so I only had to open the middle latch of the box. I took out the pop-up brush, the silver chain link, and the sharpened pencil and stuffed them all in my pants pocket. The severed green rose laid on the brown wood bottom of the box.

I closed the lid of the box and placed it on the ground. I walked over to Isabel to pick up the hammer. I gripped it in my right hand and approached the box.

I took a deep breath, grasped the hammer with both hands, and smashed the box into bits. I pounded a half dozen hits on the box until it was reduced to chunks and bits of wood. The severed head of the rose seemed to have vanished or at least buried with the rest of the rubble.

I dropped the hammer and walked over to sit next to Isabel. She flashed that same ebullient smile she always did, a smile I would always cherish. She took another long gaze up at the star-speckled sky. I wondered if she was used to looking up at the stars, or if this time, they showed her something she had never seen before. She hummed and turned her attention back to me. She put her warm hand on my shoulder.

"You will know enlightenment when it comes to you. You are your own teacher. I am part of you as much as you are part of yourself."

My body felt frozen, but I didn't have the urge to unthaw myself. I was stunned by her message. Her reverence. It was a pleasant feeling. A warmth I used to feel by my side slowly faded.

Instead, it rushed into my body, filling every vessel it could inject itself into. Whatever concept of time I previously held was shattered to smithereens. The brushing of the tree branches stopped as the air itself seemed to have completely paused in place. I felt an indescribable sense of comfort and understanding. I looked up in the sky to gaze at the white glow of the crescent moon.

I was alone sitting on the steps, trying to calm my mind and put it back to relative submission. The stillness of everything around me started to melt away. The trees started to sway as the air blew through their branches. What previously felt warm was now cold. I looked around the courtyard. I could see a thin layer of frost covering the dirt, the leaves on the trees, on the cement steps. With every exhale, I released a cloud of vapor into the air. Everything around me was cold, but my body—everything inside of me— was warm.

The cold is temporary.

I have found a better understanding of myself. I have made progress that I could deem authentic and part of a progression toward who I want to be.

This was part of my journey of self-discovery. But adding the word "self" felt confusing. But it was, truly, myself. *It was all me.* And the personification of my subconscious was a testament to my self-discovery.

But I was still surprised, because I never knew my understanding would come in the form of someone I hold near and dear to my heart. Someone I would never want to disappoint.

HELP

When Isabel was at the lowest point in her life, raising me and my brother kept her alive. She had so much darkness inside of her from her upbringing and the abusive relationship she had to endure. She had no idea if her life would ever give her meaning and fulfillment.

We ended up becoming her salvation, and for 23 years, I had no idea how much I meant to this woman, pulling her out of the despairs of her own life before I could even chew solid foods. But in the same breath, I can say that she has imprinted on me more than anyone in my life.

But why did I listen to Isabel? Why not anyone else? Why *her* specifically?

Because the love Isabel gave me was downright preposterous. Nothing was asked for in return, and nothing was asked for in general. Isabel loved, knowing that her return would net zero. Her blind altruism is rivaled by anything I've ever known, since for the longest time, I believed that people helped others by carrying out acts of kindness, generosity, and love for an extrinsic return, whether immediate or long-term.

But Isabel smashed that perception to bits. We talk about amazing women in the C-suite who wear blazers and automatically redeem the title of "girl boss," but to me, this is a woman I truly admire, one who can sacrifice her own life to give it to another.

Isabel never had kids. She never dated or remarried after her abusive relationship. She gave up everything to give a better life to a pair of boys she couldn't genetically call her own. She left her close family and relatives to find a new meaning in life.

Life is fundamentally a maladaptive one-player game that doesn't allow the option of adding a second controller. A lot of life consists of floating around in this existential crisis of wanting to be loved, but I didn't understand a crucial part— to live a life where I loved so much. In the beginning years of her life, Isabel felt betrayed. But she flipped around her thinking to start loving instead of craving the love of others.

In turn, she is loved by me, my brother, my parents, my entire immediate family, and so many countless others.

This process wasn't only about improving myself. If it was, I'd end up lonelier and even more isolated. I don't want to leave without first becoming someone I want to be. No matter how hopeless I feel, I understand that I have so much more time to help myself. And that change doesn't have to be a singular effort.

If I feel helpless, I'll help someone else. So much of my life was lived through the mentality of always needing something instead of always *giving* something. I genuinely didn't know how to make myself a better person, but helping someone else did.

My pains are not just about myself. I'm not entitled to any form of cure, happiness, fulfillment, or even enlightenment. But I am obligated to pay it forward and contribute to something greater than myself.

Help was the last belief I wanted to understand, but it didn't need discourse, and I felt like Isabel knew that, too. She already aided in my understanding through her direct actions for the first 15 years of my life (and thereafter) with her love, honesty, care, and knowledge.

In an epiphanic moment, a single beautiful green rose sprouted from her garden. The petals spun outward and flourished into beautiful concentric fashion. I stared at the rose for a bit, smiled, and walked back into the house to the sound of the artifacts jingling in my pocket.

I put them in my backpack, curled up under the covers, and closed my eyes, knowing for certain that there was a new tomorrow.

Chapter 9

Birds chirped in the distance, but the noise seeped through the cracks in the window. Adam was still knocked out, snoring like an industrial-sized buzzsaw. I could hear a cacophony of sound coming from outside— the engine of passing cars, the children running around the *pueblo*, and, as always, the shaking of the tree branches rustled by the wind. The warm air penetrated into the room like a heavy blanket.

The cold is temporary.

I rolled out of bed and pressed my feet against the cold cement floor. I had woken up with different pants than the ones I crawled into bed wearing. I was now fitted in a pair of pocketless black basketball shorts and a crisp white T-shirt.

I walked into the main room to be greeted by a vacant chill. Nobody was at the table and the kitchen was deserted. I nudged the door of Isabel's bedroom to find a perfectly made bed with nobody sleeping in it. I sat at the table for a moment to gather my thoughts.

Maybe I was still in a state of delirium from last night, I thought to myself. Probably not. Everything felt so real. I pressed my cold feet into the concrete floor. I rested my hands on the wood table.

The air was as pure as always— *this was real.*

I decided to shake everything off and go through my normal morning routine. Going to the bathroom to pop out my retainer (which I won't stop wearing until I'm buried into the ground), shower, brush my teeth, and wash my face. I popped back into the room, threw some clothes on, and walked back into the main room. In the distance, I could hear a car pulling up to the gate from the main road, but it wasn't just any car, it was a five-seater Volkswagen sedan. I could see the car through the rails of the smaller gate. Lupita and Tony popped out the driver and front seat.

I ran outside and asked where Isabel was, and they pointed to the back kitchen where she made her homemade tortillas. I rushed over, and of course, Isabel was there, dicing onions, chopping tomatoes, mincing meats, and crushing chilis to make salsa. But it wasn't just her. Isabel was armed with a small armada of eight other women helping her prepare all the ingredients for a large feast. I was disoriented.

"Isabel! What's going on? Why all the food?" Isabel turned around and audibly gasped with excitement to see me finally awake. To her, it was as if I had woken up from a coma.

"Sammy!" She dropped everything and gave me a koala bear hug. "We are preparing a celebration!" She released me and went back to dicing the august. I scratched my head. It was August. Mexican Independence Day wasn't until September and Día de Muertos didn't start until late October.

"What celebration?" I asked.

Isabel smiled and turned to me while still dicing the onions.

"'Ets a special day!"

She refused to tell me. I assumed it was a goodbye celebration, since Adam and I would be boarding our plane back home later in the afternoon, but it was more than that. Adam had woken up by this time and also came outside to see what had unfolded. He was just as confused as I was.

Slowly, one by one, people started to fill the courtyard. Nieces, nephews, brothers, sisters, and friends of Isabel's started to pour in. The men brought over the equipment: long spools of green rope, long green pipes, green folding chairs, tables, and an enormous green and white striped tarp. They immediately got to work, tying the rope to the sturdy trees in Isabel's courtyard and using the pipes to lift the tarp in an upside-down 'V' shape. They set up the tables and chairs all under the tarp and cracked open the first case of Corona bottles when the dining area was complete.

The women accompanied Isabel in the back kitchen to help with preparing the food. Buckets and plates of meats, veggies, fruits, and spices were scattered all over the back kitchen. We brought them a case of Corona beer for them to enjoy while they continued to prepare the food.

"Oh my God," was all that Adam could say as he recorded all the Oaxacan women on his phone preparing a behemoth of a feast.

"You guys need some beers!" he exclaimed, bringing all the women ice-cold Coronas with a smile as warm as Grandma's knitted sweater.

We then both sat under the canopy with the rest of the men. We popped Coronas and tried to talk as much as we could in Spanish. Most of them, like Lupita and Tony, had limited English, so our conversations were very simple, but nonetheless enjoyable.

Everyone was surprised by our visit. There was a mystical aua in the air. To them, we seemed like urban legends. They all heard about us from Isabel, but never thought in a million years we would actually come to visit.

The feast was ready. Plates filled with hearty steak and tossed salad cluttered the table. The women sat down with their men and everyone dug into their meals. The atmosphere was filled with talking, laughing, the clanking of beer bottles, and the ebullient yelling of the children playing with each other. A cool breeze blew through the courtyard, rustling the branches of the trees and causing the turkeys to gobble as they sat behind their wire fence enclosure.

Isabel came and sat with us, her heart full of warmth and complacency. While many people have to fly hundreds of miles to see the people they care about, Isabel's *barrio*-style neighborhood gives her the ability to feel the warmth and company of all her family just by walking a couple of steps in any direction.

They're happy and fulfilled to be at home within arms-reach of each other. They loved large family gatherings and had a preferred taste for Corona (which is akin to drinking a bottle filled with half beer and half water). Isabel found fulfillment, became much happier, and surrounded herself with people who love her dearly. In a nutshell, Isabel found her identity, pulled herself out of deep isolation, and reframed her ideology toward a more optimistic view of the world.

Isabel became my true Mandarin.

The feast wrapped up and Isabel instructed me to stay seated while the women cleared the plates off the table. From inside the house, Lupita came out with a giant chocolate cake with "Happy Birthday, Sam" inscribed in bright blue frosting.

I had completely forgotten it was my birthday. Everyone sang Feliz Cumpleaños, Adam pushed my head into the cake, and we continued to enjoy ourselves. Here I was, celebrating the day of my birth, surrounded by a loving community of people I had only met two hours ago.

This was my favorite birthday.

The celebration came to a close. Adam and I helped Isabel clear the plates and dump them into the kitchen. I grabbed a stack of 15 from the table and as I was entering the house, I glanced over at the garden. The green rose had vanished. I looked down and saw a visible hole in the ground, as if the stem was yanked out of the soil.

My arms started to wobble from the weight of the plates, so I went inside to dispose of them. Isabel was already washing some of the dishes as I placed my stack next to the sink. Again, my attention was caught by the photos on the fridge— specifically, the same one from the first day. That baby blue outfit, my jubilant smile, Isabel's look of dismay. I stopped in place for a moment to look at it again. Isabel noticed this and shut off the water. She walked over to look at the photo.

"Your brother, he cry and yell so much! But you, Sammy, you were so quiet! You deedn't cry and you deedn't even smile. But I love 'dees photo so much because you are so happy! And I knew at that moment, you were my special one."

The feast came to a close as our departure time slowly crept up on us. We said our goodbyes and our clan of five left for the airport in the five-seater Volkswagen sedan.

At the airport, Isabel gave both of us the strongest hugs she could muster. Before I was about to enter the security line, Isabel told me one last thing.

"The most important thing for you is to live the best you can! Sammy, I want you to get 'dees help if you need it. I want you to enjoy 'dis life you have!"

For the longest time, I believed true intellect had to have the right appearance, but Isabel shattered that perception for me. She didn't have any degrees, books, publications, or accolades. Isabel is poor in material wealth, but she's rich in knowledge. There isn't a true way for me to measure her intellect. The only way is to listen to it first-hand.

And I did.

———

The intercom blared, "Flight 364 with service to Los Angeles is now boarding."

Adam was flying back to San Diego at a different gate in the airport, so I was by myself. I sat up and waited in line to board the plane. My stomach growled, so I ran over to one of the snack kiosks and paid for a strawberry power bar. It was $3.99. It was a rip-off and the cashier gave me a "what can you do?" face as she swiped my credit card.

I devoured the bar in line and forgot I needed to make an important call. The intercom blared the same message again. For a moment, I closed my eyes and tuned out all the noise in the airport terminal.

Isabel took her flight 26 years ago— a decision that would ultimately provide her with peace and fulfillment.

It was time for me to get on the plane and take off at one place and land at another. I exhaled and walked onto the jet bridge.

I got off the plane and walked out to the pickup zone. Then, a car horn blared three times. I swiveled my head and saw the beige 2005 Honda Odyssey. The doors swung open and I jumped in.

"Welcome back!" Martin beamed. "Don't worry. You ain't missed shit!"

We drove out of the terminal and onto the main highway. I told him about my trip— the historical sites we visited, the Oaxacan food I ate. I didn't share anything else. Martin was ecstatic. He told me about his cousin's wedding and the drunk college student he had to kick out of his Uber for spilling BBQ sauce on the upholstery.

We pulled up to my apartment, but before he dropped me off, Martin showed me his phone. "I almost forgot! Take a look at this."

It was his earnings displayed in the Uber app for drivers. It was $710.

"I took your advice, and guess what," he said. "None of it went to scratchers." He pulled down the driver's side visor above his head where no scratchers had been stuffed.

"Taco Bell's got some nice stalls. I'll tell you that much." I congratulated him and thanked him for the ride. He waved and slowly drove off. No tire marks this time.

DAY 327

I walked into the doctor's office and up to the cute receptionist sitting behind the large opaque desk. She wore thick black glasses that reflected the glare of her computer screen.

"Do you have an appointment?" she asked.

"I do. For Sam at 2:30."

She clacked the keys on the keyboard and instructed me to take a seat. I walked over to one of the flimsy plastic chairs with a checkered colored cushion and sat down, looking at those beige-colored walls with paintings you would see in a nursing home.

I unraveled my backpack straps and laid it on the floor. I flashed on my phone screen— *6 MESSAGES IN YOUR INBOX.*

They were all from Isabel.

It only took traveling 2,000 miles to rekindle my appreciation for her. We had been talking regularly and she was getting the hang of using WhatsApp on her phone. She was still taking care of her father in Oaxaca. He refuses to relax and insists on working, even at the ripe age of 90. He still gets up early to pull out the plants and flowers in her garden, still driving her nuts.

Isabel had also just gotten my care package. It felt wrong that Isabel didn't have any current pictures of me and my family in her beautiful home. I printed out and framed pictures of me, Adam, my parents, and the rest of the family and mailed them to her. It took almost a year to get some decent photos of myself to send. Isabel was overjoyed and sent me half a dozen messages on WhatsApp.

Oh Sammy! Look at your face! Such a handsome man! What 'es 'dat on your face?

One of the pictures I sent was of me hiking in Mammoth Lakes. I had grown a full beard since we were still in quarantine from the Coronavirus outbreak. All anybody did was hike. I couldn't tell, but I could feel her physically smile through the phone.

I recorded one of our phone calls and kept it as an audio file on my computer. I'd collapse if I lost her, but if anything, I could always hear her voice. Her soft and jubilant tone. Her semi-fluent English that created some absolutely loveable pronunciations. Her aura of pure goodness.

My stomach growled, so I dug into my backpack to find a chocolate energy bar. I stuffed my hand deep inside, but I couldn't find the soft rectangular object. I dumped everything in the bag onto the carpeted floor— extra paper, sticky notes, a ruler, Ticonderoga pencil, a bike lock, an unlocked silver stainless-steel carabiner, but yet again, no chocolate energy bar. I started collecting everything.

Thankfully, I was the only one in the waiting room. The receptionist had earbuds in and continued to drum along to some 70's rock band in sweet ignorance.

"Sam," a voice from the other side of the room said. "Dr. Harding will see you now." The nurse was standing by the door holding a plastic clipboard. I had zoned out again.

I was let into the same patient room where I sat in the same chair in front of the same phoropter. It had almost been a year, and I needed another eye exam so I could buy more contacts.

Dr. Harding came in faster than last time. I didn't have the time nor the interest to analyze the room again. He gave me a friendly hello and sat at his computer, typing away. I sat uncomfortably against the stiff back of the patient chair.

"Going anywhere fun this time?" he asked.

I told him I wasn't. He smiled and swiveled his chair up to me. He put the phoropter up to my face, showing me the same blurry and sharp images and I gave him my slightly stupid guesses.

"The right eye caught up to the left," he said. "I'll bump it up to -2.75." He scribbled his John Hancock signature on the prescription slip lickity-split quick and handed it back to me. He got up from his computer and opened the door for me to leave. I got up and started to walk out into the hallway.

"You were right," he said as I was leaving.

"About what?"

"From last time you were here. You were right. Now I can see it every day I walk out of the office."

"See what? What are you talking about?"

He smiled, but was dragged into another room by one of his opticians before he could finish his sentence. I walked out of the room and down the small corridor into the waiting room. I said thank you to the receptionist in passing, and told her to have a good rest of her day.

As I pushed open the door to leave the office, I looked up and noticed something new. Sitting on top of the door frame, hung beautifully and with attentive care, was a picture frame, and inside it—the medical degree of someone he admired and loved.

You will know enlightenment when it comes to you.

I WILL SEE YOU SOON, ISABEL

THIS BOOK IS ALSO DEDICATED TO ALL MY FRIENDS AND FAMILY

THE PEOPLE THAT GIVE ME LOVE, SUPPORT, AND SOMETIMES REASONS TO PULL MY HAIR OUT

ABOUT THE AUTHOR

Sam Calvo grew up with his mother, older brother, and Isabel in Washington state. Sam completed high school with an ok GPA and a 1200 SAT score and somehow, he eventually graduated from college with a bachelor's degree in Communication. Sam does not hold a Master's or Doctorate degree in anything. Sam has never served as a clinical professor nor has he ever published any scientific papers or literature. Sam is not an internationally bestselling author and his books have not been translated into over 6,500 languages (yet). Sam currently lives in Los Angeles with his roommate that he found on Facebook and is still fond of truck-patterned pajamas.

REVIEWS ARE THE LIFEBLOOD OF THIS NOVEL

IT'S A WAY FOR ME TO HEAR YOUR THOUGHTS SO I CAN STRIVE TO IMPROVE MY FUTURE WORK. **IF YOU ENJOYED READING THIS NOVEL, PLEASE LEAVE AN *HONEST* REVIEW.**

YOUR IMPACT IS **EXTRAORDINARY.**

Made in the USA
Middletown, DE
01 July 2022

68195183R00161